W9-DGZ-471

Nassim's forces were tightening the noose

Bolan knew his team couldn't leave the compound through the hole they'd blasted in the wall—the defenders had already blocked it. The armored car had been moved just outside the gap, machine guns and cannon aimed and ready.

Bittrich raced forward with another charge of plastique. He lighted the end of the quick-burning fuse, sprinted across the open space to the wall and shoved the charge into place.

The bomb exploded with a roar, collapsing the prison wing. Running outside, Bolan saw a gaping hole in the wall, their way out.

Sokolov and Anahita led the hostages across the no-man's land between the prison and the wall. The hostages moved awkwardly, their chains whipping the ground.

Barnes and the Executioner stayed behind until everyone else was out, discouraging pursuit with quick, accurate bursts. Suddenly it was over. They were safely out of the palace grounds.

But Saravabad was alive with enemy forces moving in for the kill.

MACK BOLAN.

The Executioner

#132 The Big Kill	Stony Man Doctrine
#133 Blood Run	Terminal Velocity
#134 White Line War	Resurrection Day
#135 Devil Force	Dirty War
#136 Down and Dirty	Flight 741
#137 Battle Lines	Dead Easy
#138 Kill Trap	Sudden Death
#139 Cutting Edge	Rogue Force
#140 Wild Card	Tropic Heat
#141 Direct Hit	Fire in the Sky
#142 Fatal Error	Anvil of Hell
#143 Helldust Cruise	Flash Point
#144 Whipsaw	Flesh and Blood
#145 Chicago Payoff	Moving Target
#146 Deadly Tactics	Tightrope
#147 Payback Game	Blowout
#148 Deep and Swift	Blood Fever
#149 Blood Rules	Knockdown
#150 Death Load	Assault
#151 Message to Medellín	Backlash
#152 Combat Stretch	Siege
#153 Firebase Florida	Blockade
#154 Night Hit	Evil Kingdom
#155 Hawaiian Heat	Counterblow
#156 Phantom Force	Hardline
#157 Cayman Strike	Firepower
#158 Firing Line	Storm Burst
#159 Steel and Flame	Intercept
#160 Storm Warning	Lethal Impact
#161 Eye of the Storm	
#162 Colors of Hell	
#163 Warrior's Edge	
#164 Death Trail	
#165 Fire Sweep	
#166 Assassin's Creed	
#167 Double Action	
#168 Blood Price	

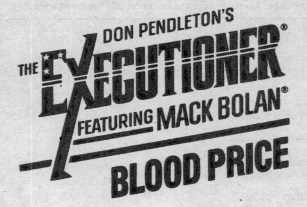

DON PENDLETON'S THE EXECUTIONER®

FEATURING MACK BOLAN®

BLOOD PRICE

A GOLD EAGLE BOOK FROM
WORLDWIDE®

TORONTO • NEW YORK • LONDON
AMSTERDAM • PARIS • SYDNEY • HAMBURG
STOCKHOLM • ATHENS • TOKYO • MILAN
MADRID • WARSAW • BUDAPEST • AUCKLAND

If you purchased this book without a cover you should be aware that this book is stolen property. It was reported as "unsold and destroyed" to the publisher, and neither the author nor the publisher has received any payment for this "stripped book."

First edition December 1992

ISBN 0-373-61168-4

Special thanks and acknowledgment to
Carl Furst for his contribution to this work.

BLOOD PRICE

Copyright © 1992 by Worldwide Library.
Philippine copyright 1992. Australian copyright 1992.

All rights reserved. Except for use in any review, the reproduction or utilization of this work in whole or in part in any form by any electronic, mechanical or other means, now known or hereafter invented, including xerography, photocopying and recording, or in any information storage or retrieval system, is forbidden without the permission of the publisher, Worldwide Library, 225 Duncan Mill Road, Don Mills, Ontario, Canada M3B 3K9.

All the characters in this book have no existence outside the imagination of the author and have no relation whatsoever to anyone bearing the same name or names. They are not even distantly inspired by any individual known or unknown to the author, and all the incidents are pure invention.

® are Trademarks registered in the United States Patent and Trademark Office and in other countries. TM are Trademarks of the publisher.

Printed in U.S.A.

Wars may be fought with weapons, but they are won by men. It is the spirit of the men who follow and of the man who leads that gains the victory.

—George S. Patton
1885-1945

In times of war a man not only has the right to kill—it becomes his duty. The innocents must be protected, no matter the cost.

—Mack Bolan

THE
MACK BOLAN™
LEGEND

Nothing less than a war could have fashioned the destiny of the man called Mack Bolan. Bolan earned the Executioner title in the jungle hell of Vietnam.

But this soldier also wore another name—Sergeant Mercy. He was so tagged because of the compassion he showed to wounded comrades-in-arms and Vietnamese civilians.

Mack Bolan's second tour of duty ended prematurely when he was given emergency leave to return home and bury his family, victims of the Mob. Then he declared a one-man war against the Mafia.

He confronted the Families head-on from coast to coast, and soon a hope of victory began to appear. But Bolan had broken society's every rule. That same society started gunning for this elusive warrior—to no avail.

So Bolan was offered amnesty to work within the system against terrorism. This time, as an employee of Uncle Sam, Bolan became Colonel John Phoenix. With a command center at Stony Man Farm in Virginia, he and his new allies—Able Team and Phoenix Force—waged relentless war on a new adversary: the KGB.

But when his one true love, April Rose, died at the hands of the Soviet terror machine, Bolan severed all ties with Establishment authority.

Now, after a lengthy lone-wolf struggle and much soul-searching, the Executioner has agreed to enter an ''arm's-length'' alliance with his government once more, reserving the right to pursue personal missions in his Everlasting War.

1

"We've got a problem," Hal Brognola said bluntly. "Hoshab Nassim has reared his ugly head and is holding a couple of hostages. One is a CIA national intelligence officer, the Agency's senior man in Southwest Asia. He's alive because they don't know who he is. If they did, they'd kill him and forget the ransom. Another guy is an operative of the Mossad. They don't know who he is, either. They think they've just got a couple of American businessmen. But if they start putting the pressure on them... Those guys know things we wouldn't want anybody to find out."

Mack Bolan stretched his legs, trying to ease the cramps he'd earned by folding his long frame into one of Brognola's uncomfortable office chairs. "You want somebody to go in and rescue them," he said dryly.

"Right you are. I figured you'd welcome the chance to settle some scores with Nassim. Civilized humanity has a lot of scores to settle with that bastard and his gang of thugs."

Bolan nodded grimly. He had in mind one score in particular: the explosion aboard Pan-Arab Air Flight 91 on the runway at Riyadh. Nassim had chortled over the deaths of 138 people, calling the mass murder "a victory for God's justice in our most holy war against all His enemies." In addition to the nineteen children who had given their lives for Nassim's "victory," a young woman had died, someone Mack Bolan would never forget.

Since Nassim seized power in Karachistan in 1985, he had joined the ranks of those ruthless dictators who were sponsors of terrorism and menaces to neighboring nations. He wasn't just a military dictator who had come to power by murdering the elderly ruler of Karachistan. He was also a religious leader, the imam of the Khariji sect of Islam. The Kharijis hated their fellow Muslims more than they hated the Christians; they hated the Saudis for holding and controlling the holy places; they hated the Shiites of Iran for not carrying their Islamic revolution far enough; they hated the Israelis for establishing a nation on the sacred soil of a former Arab state. And most of all they hated Americans for their unholy, decadent way of life.

As if he had read Bolan's thought, Brognola said, "You know, Nassim really has no quarrel with the U.S. All he wants is what he can get from us."

"And he hopes he can hold us up for a bundle."

"Yes, and quite a bundle," Brognola replied. "He's sent along his shopping list. Missiles, mostly. Ground-to-air, ground-to-ground, sea-to-air. Plus some radar equipment."

"How many hostages are there exactly?" Bolan asked.

"We know of eight. Besides our CIA man and the Israeli there's a Sudanese couple, man and wife, an Iranian, an Iraqi and two Russians. There were ten originally. Nassim made his point by killing a Pakistani and a Greek."

"Do we know where the hostages are being held?"

"We know where they were last week," Brognola replied.

The big Fed stood and pulled down a rolled map of Southwest Asia that depicted Asia from Calcutta to Baghdad, from India to Iraq. The countries lay across the map, some of the names familiar, some not—Iraq, Iran, Afghanistan, Karachistan, Baluchistan, Pakistan. They were bordered by the Persian Gulf and the Arabian Sea to the south, by the former Soviet Union and China to the north, by Saudi Arabia and the nations of the Middle East to the west, and by India to the east.

Karachistan was smaller than its neighbors Iran, Afghanistan and Pakistan. Much of the northern part of the country was trackless desert. The central part was mountainous, with peaks as high as eleven thousand feet. A lower range of mountains ran parallel to the sea and a strip of land south of those mountains, varying between twenty and fifty miles wide and nearly five hundred miles long, was watered by rains off the sea and was arable.

Brognola touched a star on the map. "Saravabad," he said, "the new capital." The city was just north of the mountain range that ran parallel to the coast. "Nassim moved the capital to put it out of reach of an assault from the sea. It's surrounded by antiaircraft missile launchers. The radar on the mountains scans every approach. There's only one airport, heavily guarded by the Karachistan Cobras—Nassim's elite guard, which is separate from the Karachistani army. Aerial recon photos show tank traps scattered over every flat field for a hundred miles. Nassim is well aware of the Rapid Deployment Force and doesn't mean to let it land."

"While a task force was moving in they'd move the hostages," Bolan observed. "Or kill them."

"Right. And Saravabad is where they are—or were last week. A diplomat from Lebanon sent word out, pinpointing the hostages in a villa on the northwest side of the city."

Brognola sighed. "The operation requires more than one man. Unfortunately Phoenix Force is on a mission in Zaire. To make matters worse, countries with hostages held by Nassim want to mount an operation of their own. The President has struck a compromise—a small international team will go in, working as a single, cohesive unit.''

''Which I inherit.''

''Give the man a cigar.''

MACK BOLAN GLANCED over his combat team. He might not have chosen some of them if he'd been in charge from the beginning, but most of them were good, and he'd developed a degree of confidence in their abilities during the two days he'd trained with them. They were tough. The only drawback was that all weren't fluent in English.

One member of the team, Anahita Behzad, was female, which under normal conditions wasn't a problem. But the warrior had to wonder if the other members of the team had confidence in her abilities, whether they'd trust her with their lives. It wasn't an ideal situation, going into battle with an unknown, but there really wasn't a choice. Anahita was invaluable to the mission—she'd lived in Saravabad for seven years and had left the city only twelve months earlier. She knew the town well, knew the surrounding countryside. No one else did. And there was no one else who could be recruited on such short notice.

Sitting among the men, dressed in a desert camouflage jumpsuit and jump boots, with her parachute pack on, and bristling with weapons, Anahita Behzad managed somehow to maintain her femininity. She had tucked her lustrous black hair inside her helmet, but some strands had escaped and hung loosely to her shoulders. Her dark eyes shifted thoughtfully from one man to another. She was appraising her companions in this risky venture, just as Bolan had.

The airplane was an Ilyushin 11-76, a swept-wing, T-tail, four-jet transport used by the Russian military. It was equipped to drop paratroops and their heavier equipment through a wide rear door. In addition it was outfitted with a twin rapid-firing 23 mm cannon that could be fired from under the tail. Like the cannon on old sailing warships, these guns were carried inside but could be quickly extended through a port to deliver a nasty surprise to a fighter coming in from behind.

The Ilyushin was overflying Karachistani territory as a scheduled airline flight. Supposedly it was Aeroflot Flight 327 from Moscow to Bombay, with an intermediate stop at Baku on the Caspian Sea. Passengers waiting at Sheremetyevo Airport, Moscow, were being told their flight was delayed by an equipment problem. Soon another 11-76 would take off for Bombay, flying passengers.

Over a high desert plateau in the northwest of Karachistan the 11-76 would descend to two thousand feet above the desert floor, and the team would jump. The 11-76 would climb quickly back to its cruising altitude and continue on to its final destination.

The plan had been formulated before Mack Bolan had become involved. He could have improved on it perhaps if there had been time, but there hadn't been. Nassim had—to use the dictator's own words—"executed two spies who had sought to frustrate the sacred purposes of the Warden Believers," meaning his bullyboy terrorist squads known commonly as WB Squads. The "trials" of others were continuing, he'd said, and more executions would follow. For "trial," Bolan read "torture," maybe followed by "confession," then by murder.

His mandate was to rescue the hostages and get them out of the country. If, in addition to that, the team could deal a blow to Nassim, so much the better. But the priority was the rescue.

THE PILOT HAD earlier cautioned about rough air as they descended toward the flat land over the northwest desert, and now the Ilyushin hit updrafts like stone walls. The airplane shook and banged. All lights were extinguished.

Bolan checked his gear. Every member of the team had been issued the same basic weapons and trained with them: SIG 550 assault rifles, equipped with bayonets and night-vision sights, and MU 50-G hand grenades.

Team members were permitted to carry a personal side arm. The Executioner had chosen his favorite, a 9 mm Beretta 93-R. He knew from experience that it was reliable and accurate. Others had mini-Uzis and a variety of other handguns, chosen because of practicality, not sentimentality.

Eight people comprised the team, the same number as the hostages in Nassim's hands. Mack Bolan, better known in some quarters as the Executioner, was in command. Mikhail Sokolov had been designated second-in-command. Anahita Behzad had been recruited as guide and interpreter. Doug McCulloch, United States Marine, had Pentagon connections and had used that influence to join the team when he heard rumors that one was being put together. Ali Maquala was the Saudi representative. His mother had perished on Pan-Arab Air Flight 91. Next was explosives technician Ardeshir Sadir, an Iranian whose family had been ruined and humiliated by the Shiites and was the sworn enemy of every form of fanaticism. Jan Huygen, a mercenary soldier for twenty years and the oldest member of the team, had been sent by the Sudanese. Kurt Bittrich, a German was their weapons technician and their expert on parachuting.

A dim light winked on, and a voice spoke on the intercom, interpreted by Sokolov. "We are descending through three thousand meters. That's three thousand meters above the desert floor, not above sea level.

We are twenty-four kilometers from the jump point, approximately. Everyone should be up and attached to the static line.''

Bittrich understood English. He was on his feet immediately, attaching the rip cord of his parachute to the wire that ran the length of the plane. With dramatic gestures he indicated that everyone should do the same. They had rehearsed, and within seconds everyone was up and hooked to the wire.

The clamshell doors opened at the rear of the aircraft, instantly decompressing the compartment to the atmospheric pressure outside. The Russian cargo crew began to push bundles toward a gaping door.

The doors slid open. As Bolan stood waiting by a side door, he looked out and down. Nothing. The night was as murky dark as it had been when he was in the cockpit at twenty or thirty thousand feet. He could see no sky above, no land below.

He had jumped before, toward landmarks or marker lights, but never just into the void with no idea of what was down there. Much depended on the navigational skills of the two Russians at the controls of the Ilyushin. Maybe too much.

Green light!

Instinctively Bolan threw himself through the doorway of the aircraft and into a nothingness that could take him to his death.

SURELY THIS WAS HELL. Sauda Sadik didn't know how many days had passed since she'd seen light, how many since her wrists had been free of the handcuffs that pinned her arms behind her back. The young woman had been told nothing of her husband's status. For all she knew he could be dead.

Sauda was naked, and she thanked God for that. If she'd been clothed, her filth would corrupt the garments. Her jailers threw buckets of water on her from time to time, which was her only means of getting clean.

Her ankles were shackled, and the chain was padlocked to a pipe in a corner of the room. She couldn't see through the blindfold that covered her eyes. A short length of rope looped around the back of her neck was tied to a piece of wood, forcing it between her teeth and holding it there like a bit in a horse's mouth, so she couldn't speak.

She knew they had photographed her and sent pictures of her to reinforce whatever demands they were making of her husband's government. Her husband, Ibrahim Sadik, was an exporter of cotton, a wealthy man and a nephew of the president of the Republic of Sudan. Ibrahim's uncle had probably seen the photographs, and only God knew if he'd still want her for Ibrahim's wife, knowing that many men had seen her nakedness. She had no idea what they were demanding for Ibrahim's release, and hers. Whatever it was, she hoped the president would give it.

Her tormentors had explained that they didn't hate her, nor any of the people they'd taken hostage. What they were doing was political, as well as religious. Her husband was a Sunni Muslim, as were the majority of the world's Muslims, and they hated that.

But if they didn't hate her, why did they treat her this way? Perhaps they'd discovered that she was an American. She'd taken the name Sauda when she married and converted to Islam. But she was from Newark, New Jersey, where her name had been Melanie Helms. Her father owned a garage and was in the business of repairing trucks. She had been reared a Christian, of sorts, and had been educated at CCNY, which was where she'd met Ibrahim.

Her background could account for her ill treatment. She hoped Ibrahim wasn't being treated the same way.

She was in constant agony. The pain was unbearable. When they took the wood out of her mouth to feed her, she begged to be allowed to stretch her arms. They shoved food into her mouth and silenced her.

Sauda didn't expect to survive. In fact, death would be a release.

Unless this was hell.

2

A strong wind buffeted Mack Bolan as he prepared to touch down on the fast-approaching ground. He bent his legs and tried to land with his heels digging into the earth, but it didn't work. He was moving too fast. He was slammed over onto his face and dragged for ten yards before he could spill the parachute.

The others were coming down around him, and he was sure that not all of them would have his luck. Somebody was going to get hurt, and there was nothing he could do about it.

He heard one guy hit the ground not far from him, heard scrambling and a grunt of pain as the wind pulled the commando along the ground. Bolan trotted toward the sound and found the guy stretched out, stunned.

The commando turned out to be Anahita Behzad. She had a knife in her hand and was cutting her parachute shrouds, muttering under her breath something that sounded like angry cursing, though in a language he couldn't understand.

"Are you hurt?" Bolan asked.

"Yes," she said. "Damn right. But not injured. *Look out!*"

A man was coming down right on top of them. Bolan scrambled up and grabbed the guy's legs. Anahita threw herself against his parachute and collapsed it. It was Sokolov, the Russian.

In a few more minutes all eight were down, and Bolan had found them all. As he'd thought, luck couldn't hold for all of them. Ali Maquala, the young Arab, had a badly broken ankle. Kurt Bittrich, the German, was unconscious with a concussion. He'd been dragged hard against a rock, and the impact had driven his helmet down against his skull.

It was too dark to find their equipment, so they had no choice but to wait for dawn, less than an hour away. Doug McCulloch, the Marine, gave two morphine tablets to Maquala, then passed over his canteen. Medical supplies had been dropped, but no one could find them now.

Bittrich began to mutter. Moments later he was conscious. He said he could move out when the rest of them did. Bolan had his doubts.

THE SUN ROSE, revealing that the team stood on a desert plateau surrounded by high mountains. It wasn't just a valley. The nearest mountains were fifty or sixty miles distant, to the east.

The ground on which they sat was the flattest on the plateau. It was rock-strewn desert bare of any vegetation except a few tough, scrawny weeds. No more than a mile or so away the land rose in low ridges. The Russian pilots had dropped the team on the most suitable ground for many miles. The operation had been well planned, except that no one had anticipated the hard wind that had blown Ali and Bittrich against the rocks that injured them—and that had also blown away their parachuted equipment and supplies.

As the sun climbed higher, the bitter cold of desert night turned to the scorching heat of a desert day. McCulloch, who'd gone scouting, returned loaded with two big packs: one of food and water, one of ammunition. He headed out again, accompanied by Huygen. They came back twenty minutes later with a broken-open pack of medical supplies.

Jan Huygen was a ruddy-faced man with a blond mustache and a receding hairline. He'd soldiered everywhere: Africa, Southeast Asia and Latin America. Over the years he'd picked up many skills, among them those of a rough-and-ready medic. He knelt beside Maquala, injected his leg with a local anesthetic, set the broken ankle and taped a splint to it.

"Sorry, mate," he said, "can't make a cast. Haven't got the necessary, you understand. But I'll slice your boot to make room for the splint and we'll tie it tight. Won't be able to put your weight on it, I'm afraid."

Maquala stared at Bolan. "You'll have to leave me."

Bolan shook his head. "No way."

"Chief!"

McCulloch was yelling from a hundred yards away. None of the team had been told exactly who Bolan was, and he'd merely said to call him Striker. McCulloch, for reasons of his own, chose to call him Chief.

Bolan trotted across the rocky land to where the man squatted beside a broken pack. The Marine had found their radios, smashed. They'd have no communication. In another pack that had fallen twenty yards farther were six Armbrusts, disposable, hand-held missile launchers.

The Executioner returned to the group and gathered them around. "We can't just sit here." He swung his arm around, pointing to the most distant of the mountains. "That's south. We've got to cross those mountains and a valley on the other side. Nassim's new capital is on the slopes of the next mountain chain, and that's where the hostages are. It's quite a hike to Saravabad. That's the job we bought, and we have to get moving."

"I'll help Ali," McCulloch offered.

"As will I," Ardeshir Sadir added.

"Everybody not helping carries an Armbrust," Bolan stated, heaving an extra pack of ammo onto his shoulders. "So let's go."

THE SUN BURNED DOWN on them mercilessly. Their combat fatigues, which hadn't provided enough protection against the cold of the night, were stifling and soaked with sweat. Because they didn't know how far they'd have to go to find water, the team sipped sparingly from their canteens. The straps that held their weapons and gear chafed their shoulders. Their helmets became almost too hot to touch.

Their only relief was in the shadows of rocks. Bolan called frequent halts, and at first they sat in the shade to rest.

The Executioner studied his map, which showed a riverbed half a day's march to the west. Anahita Behzad had said a riverbed like that was dry two-thirds of the year and might well be dry now. At best it would contain some brackish ponds. The first running water they were likely to come across would be a stream, coming from the mountains and requiring a two-day march to the south.

"The water just spreads out on the land," she said, "and is soaked in. Rivers like that feed little lakes. The water is usually only a few centimeters deep. Even so, everything comes to drink."

"Including men," Bolan said.

She nodded. "Including men."

"And men are what we don't want to see."

IN MID-AFTERNOON when the sun was at its worst, Ardeshir Sadir suddenly yelled. He'd walked a little to the left of the team, intending to relieve himself.

Bolan raced to him. Sadir stood wide-eyed, staring at the ground. A viper, about three feet long, stared back with cold eyes, its tongue flicking in and out. Sadir carried a mini-Uzi as well as his SIG 550, and he lowered the muzzle toward the snake, then glanced at Bolan.

The Executioner shook his head. "It'd be heard for miles."

Sadir took a step backward, which seemed to satisfy the snake. It turned and slithered away.

"In a way it is good," Sadir said, nodding solemnly.

"Why?"

"A creature like that eats small animals," Sadir replied. "Where there are small animals there is water. Also, the snake doesn't travel far. There must be water near."

Bolan nodded. "Fresh water, too." He glanced around. "Could be a mile in any direction. We're not short of water and won't be for another day or so. But it's good to know there's water. If we had to have it, we could spread out and look for it."

They plodded along again in single file. Heat waves rising from the desert floor made the distant mountains seem to shimmer. Twice Bittrich fell. He insisted that his concussion wasn't bothering him, that only the wobbly mountains made him dizzy.

It was easy to imagine you saw all kinds of things: not mirages but the dust plumes of moving vehicles, the whirling blades of low-flying helicopters, the smoke of fires, clusters of mud buildings... Imagination played complicated tricks in the shimmering heat.

But not this time.

"Helicopter!" Sokolov yelled.

"Scatter! Get down!" Bolan yelled.

The chopper was coming straight for them, not more than a hundred feet above the ground, so low, in fact, that its blades kicked up dust. It was a military helicopter, armed, armored and fast.

Bolan rolled onto his back and sighted an Armbrust on the big chopper. If it was going to fire on the team, it would have to slow down, and when it did, it was going to get a nasty surprise. The Armbrust was meant to stop a tank. It would take out a chopper handily—if he could hit it.

The helicopter came on, looming larger every second, the downward wash from its rotor blades kicking up sand and dust. Bolan glanced at his commandos. Everyone was flat on the ground, their weapons aimed at the helicopter. But the team knew enough not to fire unless fired upon.

In seconds the chopper swept overhead, whipping them with dust, filling their eyes, noses and mouths with sand, deafening them with its harsh roar. And then suddenly it was gone. Apparently no one in the chopper had so much as noticed them.

"Find whatever cover you can!" Bolan instructed. "He could be making a sweep and may be back."

Behzad was on her knees, staring at the chopper through binoculars. "It's the Warden Believers," she said. "I can see the insignia. Not the Karachistan Cobra Force or Nassim's bullyboys."

"Looking for us?"

"One helicopter? I doubt it. I don't think Nassim knows about us yet. If he did, there'd be a score of choppers crisscrossing the desert. Look."

The helicopter was flying a circle now, a mile away. Suddenly they saw the winking bright-orange muzzle-flashes of a machine gun firing from the fuselage and the dust plume behind a speeding vehicle, charging across the desert toward them.

The driver whipped his vehicle from side to side to avoid rocks and holes, and in doing so made himself a difficult target for the machine gunner in the helicopter. Bolan took binoculars from his kit and focused on the jolting, rocking vehicle, which was a

Range Rover. The helicopter followed its course, rocking from side to side.

Machine gun slugs were being fired perilously close to the team's position. The chopper's gunner was desperately trying to hit the swerving vehicle.

It was no contest. Sooner or later the Range Rover was going to be hit.

A stream of slugs stitched the ground among the rocks where Bolan's team was crouching. And the Range Rover came on, ever closer.

"All right! That's enough!" Bolan raised the Armbrust.

The team opened fire on the chopper. Streams of 5.56 mm slugs pinged off its armored body, a few punching through the Plexiglas windows. The pilot banked his aircraft so that his machine gunner could challenge whoever dared to fire on one of Hoshab Nassim's helicopters.

That made him a perfect target for the Executioner.

The chopper was only about 150 yards away and no more than two hundred feet above the ground when Bolan pulled the trigger. The missile, fire in its tail, flew straight and fast. It broke through the armored skin of the helicopter and exploded. The machine gunner was blown out the door and fell to the ground. The body of the aircraft puffed out, and pieces of sheet metal fell off the frame. Then the big ship slowly turned nose down and plummeted to the earth, where it was consumed in a fireball.

The Range Rover stopped, both doors opened and two people climbed out. The man who had been driving raised his arms and screamed something.

Behzad walked forward and immediately they began to talk in what Bolan guessed was Urdu. They conversed and gesticulated for a full three minutes before the woman walked back to Bolan and explained.

"His name is Suleiman Zabara," she said, "and her name is Raima."

"Raima..." Bolan repeated. The young woman was beautiful—petite, with black hair and dark eyes.

"Suleiman Zabara is her father." Behzad paused before she added, "Raima is Hoshab Nassim's fourth wife. She couldn't bear to live with him. Her father was helping her escape. And Nassim would rather she die than escape from him. So...the helicopters. You see?"

Bolan glanced at the sky. "Then there'll be others coming."

"Probably. But if the vehicle isn't moving, not sending up a plume of dust, they won't find it. There is a saying: 'The desert and the sky are as big as each other.'"

Bolan shrugged. "I'd rather put a mile between us and that Range Rover just the same. What do they want to do?"

"They'll take Ali—and Bittrich if he wants to go—and make a run for the Iranian frontier after dark."

"Nassim has some sophisticated equipment," Bolan told her. "One thing he has, I'd guess, is heat-sensing scanners. It'll be cold tonight, and the engine in that Range Rover will create heat that will broadcast its position to any aircraft flying overhead."

"They can—"

"They'll have to travel a hundred miles across a desert with no roads, and they'll have to run with lights on. If Ali wants to go with them, that's his business. I'll explain it to him."

"I'll explain it to Suleiman Zabara," Behzad replied.

Bolan led his team away from the Range Rover and the crashed helicopter. They were scars on the desert and would be visible to aircraft. To be close wasn't a good idea.

In a few minutes Behzad came to him. "Suleiman Zabara asks to be allowed to come with us. He and his daughter hate Nassim. Besides, she knows something about the hostages. I think we should take them with us."

"They have to keep up," Bolan warned.

"They will."

COLONEL PAVEL ILINSKY dipped into some unappetizing tinned meat, digging it out with his fingers and stuffing it into his mouth only because he was hungry, not because it was in the least palatable.

It was odd that they should have brought him food at the hour of prayer. He could hear them outside, chanting. He couldn't see them, but he knew how they did it: on their knees, pressing their foreheads to the floor. It was odd that they let him profane their holy hour by eating.

He sat on the Spartan cot they'd provided him with. His right leg was chained to a heavy fragment of steel girder almost a meter long. He could move around, but he wasn't going far and certainly not fast.

Even so he was better off than poor Kamensky. The last time he had seen him, the man's ankles had been chained together so closely that all he could do was hobble awkwardly in short, painful steps when he went down the corridor to the toilet.

Ilinsky had never met Nikolai Kamensky before they were thrown together here in this villa somewhere in the vicinity of Saravabad. They'd been put in the same room at first because they were Russians, the only two taken in the hijacking. Ilinsky was an officer of Russian Intelligence, traveling on official business and had been on his way to Karachi, then Hyderabad. Kamensky was a minor functionary in the Ministry of Agriculture on his way to Teheran. For several days now Ilinsky hadn't seen Kamensky, and he wondered if they'd killed the man.

The colonel couldn't imagine that *he* would be injured. The bastards wouldn't dare! Twenty years ago they would have been— Well, twenty years ago was twenty years ago, when Moscow was feared. *Feared!* When the motherland knew how to deal with the scum of the earth. Now...things had changed so much that he hadn't told them he was an intelligence agent. His passport didn't say he was, so they didn't know. Yet.

The colonel grimaced as he sucked the last of the greasy meat from his fingers. He had no doubt at all that someone was on the way to rescue him.

3

The Warden Believers took about an hour to find their downed helicopter. When they did, they mustered every available aircraft and swarmed over the desert like angry hornets. Some pilots fired nervously on whatever they thought they saw, likely as not the dust devils churned up by their own rotors.

Bolan had his team spread out and hide as best they could on land that offered little in the way of cover. One burst of gunfire ricocheted off some rocks and came within a few yards of Jan Huygen and Ali Maquala. Otherwise, the sporadic bursts posed little threat.

The higher flying jets that streaked by gave Bolan more cause for concern. If they were well enough equipped, they could detect living bodies on the desert floor, which was why he'd insisted the team spread out—and at random. If the jets carried sensors that "saw" living creatures, they might take randomly spaced men and women for animals.

After the helicopters quit their firing, two landed beside the wreckage of the aircraft brought down with the Armbrust. Sokolov raced in a crouch toward Bolan and dropped beside him. "What do you suppose they'll think?" he asked. "Can they be stupid enough not to see that helicopter was brought down by a missile?"

"Right now it's just a pile of tangled metal. Could have just crashed. Unless they're experts they won't be able to figure it out."

"Let us hope they don't. If they decide that chopper was shot down, they'll send the whole Karachistan Cobra Force out here."

All Bolan's group could do was to keep down and keep quiet.

After a quarter of an hour, the choppers lifted off and clattered away. Bolan got up and led the team south.

Behzad hurried to the head of the column, bringing along Suleiman Zabara and his daughter. "I've been talking with them," she said to Bolan. "Raima says Nassim will kill all the hostages at the first hint someone is attempting a rescue. She says he himself lives part of the time in the villa where they're being held. He doesn't sleep at the presidential palace, doesn't eat there except when he receives official visitors. He thinks any attempt to assassinate him would come as an attack on the palace, likely from the air. So he moves around, doesn't go near the palace at night. He moves with a troop of about twenty bodyguards, all heavily armed. She says we should move in to save the hostages when Nassim and his guard aren't there."

For a while they trudged on in silence, the big warrior heavily burdened with his weapons and equipment, and sweating heavily in the relentless heat of the white sun. He noticed that his three companions made no complaints as they walked along. Behzad carried less than he did, but it was still a heavy load.

Zabara had shouldered someone's pack, maybe Maquala's. He was a man of fifty years, Bolan judged. His beard and mustache were iron-gray, his eyes deeply lined. He wore a double-breasted gray suit, a white shirt buttoned to his collar and a white keffiyeh that covered his head and shielded the back of his neck.

The only problem Zabara was going to have was with his shoes. They'd never take a hundred-mile march across this kind of terrain. Obviously his feet hurt already. He said nothing, but he was picking his steps carefully, trying to avoid sharp rocks.

Raima for some reason was dressed in combat fatigues. Though petite, she had relieved somebody of the weight of an Armbrust, also of an equipment belt, which she wore draped over her shoulders. She was wiry and tough and provoked a myriad questions in the Executioner's mind.

As THE SUN DROPPED, the temperature on the desert began to fall rapidly. The team had reached a wadi, a dry streambed that ran full with rushing water when rain fell in the mountains. The bottom was sandy and flat, and Bolan decided it was as good a place as any to make camp for the night. The wadi was shown on his map, and he was encouraged to see they'd covered more than twenty miles on their first day's march through the desert.

Kurt Bittrich declared that he was fully recovered from his concussion, but Bolan noticed that the man swallowed two morphine tablets as soon as they settled down. Ali Maquala had managed the arduous trek, but it had taken its toll. He, too, gulped morphine tablets, even before he ate, and was half out of it before Jan Huygen pulled off his boots and examined the swollen ankle. Huygen, after his fashion, said nothing, but walked over, sat down beside Bolan and shook his head.

The light faded. Everyone ate and drank sparingly from the canteens that now had two more people to sustain. They settled down in the sand, finding the best spots they could to rest their aching muscles. Bolan set sentries. No one was to show a light.

The warrior himself slept three hours. He'd given himself the sentry shift when a man would find it most difficult to stay awake. He, Huygen and McCulloch took that midnight watch.

The night was clear in a way that a man rarely saw in most parts of the world. Here they were hundreds of miles from the industrial nations and their stacks, and the sky was jet black with more stars glittering than anyone usually saw. Bolan remembered nights like this in various parts of the world. A man who hadn't experienced it couldn't believe it.

The temperature was below freezing now. That was the desert. He had experienced that before, too.

A helicopter clattered past, not very high, heading due north, and a dark figure moved toward him. He tensed and drew his bayonet from its scabbard. But it was Anahita Behzad. She approached him cautiously, whispering her name. He returned the bayonet to its scabbard, and she sat on the ground beside him.

"I'd give a lot to be able to light a cigarette," she said.

"Someone could see it from a hundred yards or more."

"I know."

She'd left her helmet on the ground where she'd been sleeping. Her hair hung to her shoulders, and she didn't look like a soldier.

"We're probably going to get killed, you know," she said calmly.

Bolan didn't respond.

"Did anyone explain to you why I volunteered for this job?"

"No."

"I can show you scars," she said. "I'd have to undress to show you, so you'll probably never see them. I'm Iranian. When Khomeini overthrew the Shah and the Shiite fanatics took control, my husband and I left Teheran. I should say we *fled* Teheran. My husband was an electronics engineer. Both of us were educated outside the country and we lived like modern people. We came to Karachistan. Under the previous ruler it was a good place to live. Then Nassim murdered the old man and overthrew his government. His Khariji fanatics made Karachistan worse than Iran. We couldn't leave, either. Nassim decided my husband was a valuable man. He forced him to work on the radar, also on the new broadcasting stations he set up in Saravabad.

"One day I was arrested by a squad of Khariji morals police. I was driving my car, wearing a skirt that was well below my knees but didn't cover my ankles. A traffic policeman had seen my ankles and reported to the morals squad that I had offended and embarrassed him. I was whipped. I saw my own blood spatter on the wall. When my husband came to the station to take me home, he complained loudly about what had been done to me. One of the policemen hit him with brass knuckles. It broke his jaw and destroyed some of his teeth.

"We still couldn't leave. We were prisoners in Karachistan. My husband had to go on working for Nassim, and I had to wear the chador. Then last year my husband died. A week later they handed me my passport and told me to get out of the country. I burn with hate. Can you understand?"

"I can understand very well. I didn't choose to do what I do because of kindness and gentleness in the world."

She sighed. "Don't worry about me. I won't let my anger drive me to do something foolish."

The warrior touched her shoulder. While she was talking he had noticed something. The stars near the horizon to the east were disappearing and reappearing. Something was moving on the desert just beyond the edge of the wadi.

Behzad stiffened under his touch. Maybe she thought he was making an advance. Then she saw what he was pointing at.

"You know where Huygen and McCulloch are?" he whispered. "Alert them. Tell them not to fire a shot unless it's absolutely necessary."

"Could be a stray camel," she suggested.

"Could be." But he didn't think so. The movement he saw was too regular, too much in a straight line, too purposeful. Once again he drew his bayonet from its scabbard, and Behzad slipped away into the darkness at the bottom of the shallow streambed.

He judged he might be looking at three men. It was all but impossible to tell, but the shadows that moved across the pattern of stars in the east looked like three.

If this was a force, sent because the choppers had spotted his little group, why only three men? Or were they scouts, a few men from a larger force searching the wide desert?

He decided not to awaken the rest of his team. If they faced only a few men, he, Huygen and Mc-Culloch should be able to handle them. With more people awake, including the inexperienced Suleiman Zabara and his daughter, there was a greater chance for confusion. Also, the more awake the more likely a shot would be fired—and that was something he wanted to avoid.

The wadi was no more than four feet deep. Bolan slipped to the eastern bank and crouched, waiting for one of the intruders to approach.

He thought he heard another one of his commandos moving in the same direction, but he couldn't be sure.

Then Bolan spotted a man at the edge of the bank about ten yards south. The intruder jumped, landing in the bed of the wadi and pausing for a long moment. He seemed to be looking around, taking stock, seeing if anyone was awake. He moved silently then across the sand toward the sleeping members of the combat team.

Bolan was behind him. The warrior could see the man better now, could judge him. He wore some sort of uniform jacket, loose pants and a keffiyeh. He carried a rifle—an assault rifle from the look of it.

The intruder stopped beside one of the sleeping men and glanced around, though not all the way behind him. Then he bent his knees, laid his rifle on the ground and drew a knife from his belt.

Bolan didn't need to see more. Moving forward with one quick step, he threw his left arm around the man's neck and with his right drove the point of the bayonet into this throat. The man struggled for a few seconds, then went limp.

The Executioner crouched, staring hard into the darkness, listening. If the small sound of the attack had alerted anyone, there was no sign of it.

But someone knew what had transpired and scrambled on hands and knees across the wadi. It was Behzad. "I told them," she whispered, glancing at the body. "They are alert."

Anahita nudged the warrior. She'd heard the muffled thud of booted feet. Bolan had heard it, too—another man had dropped into the wadi. That man lived about fifteen seconds after he hit the sand. Bolan didn't know if it was Huygen or McCulloch who got him, but the man gasped as a bayonet cut his throat.

The Executioner trotted to the edge of the wadi and heaved himself up onto the floor of the desert as quietly as he could. The high ground. If the other attacker hadn't jumped into the wadi yet, there was a chance to get him up there.

Bolan squatted, peered at his surroundings and saw the third man silhouetted against the stars. This man was different. He stood six feet or more and wore a robe. He strode to the edge of the wadi, obviously to survey what his two men had accomplished below.

Bolan slipped around and came up behind him. In an instant the warrior's bayonet was pressed against his opponent's throat. The man threw his arms out to both sides in a gesture of surrender.

IN THE FIRST LIGHT of dawn Maquala hobbled painfully to the eastern bank of the wadi to see what Sadir, Zabara and his daughter were staring at.

Two dead men lay stretched out in front of a third, a tall, thin, black-bearded man dressed in black robes and wearing a white keffiyeh. McCulloch guarded the man, who stared at him with hate-filled eyes.

"Who is that?" Maquala asked.

"Sayed Masoud."

"And who is Sayed Masoud?"

"It depends on who you ask," Sadir replied. "He calls himself a noble chief. Most people call him a bandit. His tribe is called the Masoudi. They have never been anything but bandits."

Maquala stared thoughtfully at the chief, who stared back with an evil glint in his eyes.

"An enemy of Nassim should be a friend of ours," Sadir stated, "but this one is not. In the old days Masoud rode the desert on a white camel, robbing when he chose, raping when he chose, and the Masoudi were rich. Nassim has reduced them to poverty. They are rats, he and his followers, scrounging what they can. He saw us enter this wadi last night and came to kill us and take what he could. He didn't know how many we were or that we are soldiers." He pointed to the bodies. He sent these two into the wadi to murder us in our sleep. They would have done it, too, except that we are led by a masterful soldier and are served by others. While we slept this trash came to attack...and died for their crime."

Sayed Masoud didn't understand a word of English. He glared at the speakers, aware of their scorn and himself scornful.

A few yards away Bolan and Sokolov talked with Behzad. "I don't have any idea how many men he leads," she told the men. "The Masoudi would still be a hundred men at least. They'll be looking for him now."

"A desert bandit," Sokolov mused.

"Always," Behzad said. "As his father was, also his grandfather. Waste no sympathy on him, Striker. He misjudged us. He meant to kill us all, however many we might be, and steal whatever we had. He thought he'd seen a group of three or four. He had no idea who we are or what we are. He would have enjoyed finding two women among us.

"There's only one way to take care of the problem of Sayed Masoud," she said grimly.

"And what's that?" Bolan prompted.

"Cut his throat. Leave the three men spread out on rocks for the vultures to pick at. When the others see that, they'll take warning."

Bolan shook his head. "I can't order a man's execution."

"Then eat and drink," Behzad said. "I suppose we're marching on south today. The sun is rising. It would be well to cover as many kilometers as we can before the heat of the day."

Bolan nodded and turned to join the others.

Moments later Bolan heard a muffled shot and jumped to his feet. He knew where it had come from.

Behzad stood over the body of Sayed Masoud, watching the last twitches of his life. She shoved her silenced Beretta back inside her jacket as Bolan reached her. She calmly nodded toward the bodies. "Our worries will be over. Leave the bodies for the desert vermin. The Masoudi will hold back when they see the remains.''

THEY DIDN'T KNOW Nathan Block was a Mossad agent. His passport identified him as an Israeli citizen, an importer of fish. He'd been on his way to Pakistan, according to his cover story, to meet with Pakistani fish exporters to negotiate an agreement. There was enough truth in the story to make it stand up if Nassim thought to inquire of the Pakistanis.

Very likely Block knew more about the many elements of his captivity and that of his fellow hostages than any of the others—more, in fact, than Nassim himself knew. He was the only hostage, almost certainly, who had actually confronted the strange, perverse dictator. He alone, as far as he knew, had been taken into the villa itself and brought face-to-face with Nassim.

He'd been carried into the small, sparely furnished office where the tyrant sat behind a small wooden desk—carried because the shackles on his ankles weren't connected by chain but by a steel bar, and he couldn't walk. He was still shackled that way and could make his way to the toilet only by a series of short hops. The chain between his wrists had been shortened by a padlock that day, and he had carried his hands clasped together.

Nassim had looked up at him. "In the name of God, the beneficent, the merciful... So. A Jew. An Israelite. I wanted to see what one looked like."

"Is that the reason I've been brought to Saravabad?" Block asked.

Nassim smiled and nodded. "As good a reason as any. Your country will concede nothing. Between us it is war to the death."

"That's exactly right."

The tyrant hadn't expected that kind of answer. His eyes flashed with surprise, then with anger.

Hoshab Nassim was a memorable man. His eyes, under great, flaring, bushy brows, burned with an inner fire. His graying beard almost concealed his mouth, but Block saw his lips stiffen with fury. The man wore a black turban and a long white cotton robe over a khaki military jacket festooned with gaudy medals. He wore jodhpurs and riding boots, and a riding crop lay on the desk beside his right hand.

Block supposed at that moment that he was about to die, even if Nassim didn't know he was an Israel intelligence agent. And there was no way of knowing that, either.

If the Arab dictator found out that the Sudanese, Ibrahim Sadik, worked for the Mossad, Block's one slim chance would be lost. Sadik's wife had been traveling with him and had been taken hostage, too. She most likely didn't know her husband worked for the Mossad and probably thought he earned his money as he said he did.

From time to time Block had heard the beautiful black woman cry out. More often he heard her groan. He wondered if they were forcing Sadik to witness the torture of his wife. If they did, he'd break. He was a good man but not that good.

It might be a good thing if Sadik somehow died. From what he heard from the adjoining cell, perhaps it would be a good thing if she did, as well.

4

Anahita Behzad was wrong in thinking the Masoudi would be scared off by the death of their chief. Two hours after Bolan led his party away from their overnight camp the tribesmen began to appear. Out in the desert, a cautious distance away, they followed the team south. What they were doing was completely obvious. Recon. They were watching, appraising, probably through binoculars. And they were gathering. An hour after their first appearance there were more than fifty of them—a ragtag crowd, some in desert robes, some in pieces of military uniform, most in the varied, tattered clothes of tribal poor.

They were split into two groups, one to the east and one to the west of the streambed Bolan was following. The group to the east was by far the bigger. A few of them were mounted on small horses. Two, both to the east, were mounted on camels.

They kept almost a mile behind. None dared approach the little column. If they had binoculars, they could see the assault rifles and the Armbrusts. And they could have no doubt this band of soldiers would kill.

Raima and her father, who now wore a pair of boots taken from a corpse, walked beside Bolan, accompanied by Behzad. He wanted to talk to them, and Behzad would interpret.

"I've got one question," Bolan said, "and it's for all three of you. How likely is it that the Masoudi will go to Nassim and report that a group of soldiers marching south killed their chief?"

Behzad translated, and Zabara spoke solemnly. "He says the Masoudi wouldn't dare go to Nassim. The Warden Believers have murdered scores of them. In fact, that's probably what they think we are—a squad of the Believers."

Raima spoke, and Behzad translated. "Nassim has sworn to exterminate the Masoudi. They are a threat to his regime."

"A hundred tribesmen are a threat to his regime?"

"He hates and is determined to destroy anyone who defies him. He'll kill me if he can . . . and my father. We're quite sure they've already demolished my father's house."

Behzad explained. "It's a sacrifice he made to save his daughter. Not many Karachistani fathers would do it."

Huygen joined them. He nodded toward their Masoudi shadows. "They make me think of one of your western movies I saw one time. The Indians hovering near a wagon train... You know?''

''I don't think they'll attack now'' Bolan replied. ''But tonight will be a different story.''

ABOUT NOON they came across pools of water standing in the wadi. The water was trickling very slowly under the sand and appearing in low places. It was brackish from minerals leached out of the sand. But a little farther along the pools were interconnected by a tiny flow running on the surface in the middle of the wadi, and a short distance beyond that they came to a pond about a hundred yards across. Water flowed from this pond into five wadis, spreading like five fingers from the palm of a hand. The arm was a mountain stream, a narrow, gurgling flow of cold, clear water.

The water was good, and they filled their canteens and splashed it over their heads. As Sadir had warned, water attracted animals, and small animals attracted predators—not just the slithering vipers they'd seen earlier but cobras and big, aggressive-looking lizards that Sadir said were harmless.

A few trees grew along the banks of the little river, affording shade, where they rested. Bolan sat in the shadow of a gnarled old tree and studied his map. From here on the job got trickier. The map showed a village a few miles to the east, on the banks of another, larger mountain stream. Several miles south was another village, lying directly in their southward line of march.

The fact was, they were moving out of the barren, sandy desert into the foothills of the Ashkab Mountains. The foothills and slopes of the mountains were no garden paradise, but they were areas where sheep and goats could graze. Bolan had to expect encounters with shepherds.

He assembled the team. "Okay," he said. "It's great to find water and to fill our canteens. Now we've got to head out. We like the water, and so do the people who live around here. We don't want to meet anybody. We want to keep our presence in this country as secret as possible as long as possible. So get everything together. We head out in five minutes."

Before they could move away from the little river though, the helicopters appeared again. This time there were three of them. They flew slowly, obviously scanning the ground.

Bolan and his team spread out and took cover under trees or in the shelter of big rocks. Sokolov had to throw rocks at a cobra and drive it out of the trench between two boulders where he wanted to hide. The choppers hovered for a moment above the mountain stream, then slowly moved on.

The Masoudi had scattered. They were nowhere to be seen.

As soon as the choppers were out of sight to the north, Bolan led his people to the west, over a rocky ridge and into a little ravine on the other side. They moved south again, patrolling the slope of the ridge they'd crossed and another to their west, moving again in dry, dusty heat. McCulloch and Huygen took the point on the two ridges, climbing near the top and advancing cautiously southward.

The Masoudi were out there again, keeping their distance but following relentlessly. It was, as Huygen had said, something like having Indians following a wagon train.

"They'll attack tonight," Sokolov stated.

Bolan nodded. He had already come to the same conclusion.

McCulloch climbed down from the ridge. "Something's out there," he said, pointing southward. "Something's in the gully, waiting for us. Let me use your binoculars so I can check it out."

Bolan handed over the binoculars, and McCulloch ran up the rough slope to the top of the ridge. He stared for a moment, then returned. "There are six bodies, propped up for us to look at."

Alerted, the combat team formed a skirmish line and moved warily forward, leaving Zabara and his daughter with Ali in a rockbound depression where they would be sheltered from Masoudi fire and could hold out until the main party returned.

They moved slowly, but beyond a small turn in the ravine they came in sight of what Doug McCulloch had reported—bodies lying on rocks, obviously laid out to be a display.

Behzad walked beside Bolan. "That's their answer to the deaths of Sayed Masoud and his two men," she said quietly.

"Who are they?" Bolan asked.

She shook her head and walked closer to the naked bodies of six men. Their throats had been slit. She looked at them closely. When Bolan came up beside her, she turned to him and said, "They're Warden Believers. See the copper bracelets? That's their insignia. Their serial numbers are stamped on them, something like the way American soldiers used to wear dog tags. Don't waste any sympathy on them. They've killed people, you can be sure."

"They were prisoners."

She nodded. "And have been for a long time. See the rope burns on their wrists and ankles? They've been kept tied."

Bolan put his binoculars to his eyes and scanned the ridge top ahead and behind. "So the Masoudi murdered their prisoners. And they're the people we'll have to fight tonight."

THIS WAS A FIGHT Bolan definitely didn't want—to face a night attack by a tribe of desert bandits. A lot of men were going to get hurt. Shots would be fired, heard by shepherds and villagers. It could destroy their mission in Karachistan.

Sokolov was inclined to blame Anahita Behzad, who had shot Masoud. "We have no quarrel with these illiterate nomads," he said.

Bolan stared at him for a brief moment. "Apart from the fact that some of them came to our camp last night and tried to kill us, you mean?"

The Executioner had no choice but to prepare his team to repel a ferocious night assault. As the sun set, he deployed his forces. He ordered Maquala, Zabara and Raima to hide in a nest of rocks, and he even moved some rocks to their position to provide better protection. Maquala refused morphine but allowed Huygen to inject a local anesthetic into his swollen ankle. The rest of the force took up stations north and south in the ravine and on its slopes, waiting for sunset.

As soon as the sun had set and it was dark, everyone moved. Obviously the Masoudi had observed their dispositions; and now that the tribesmen couldn't see them do it, the whole team, including Suleiman, Raima and Ali, moved. They went to the top of the western ridge and stretched out in positions already chosen by Bolan and Sokolov.

They had one immense advantage. Their SIG 550 assault rifles were equipped with night vision sights. The Masoudi couldn't sneak up on them in the dark.

On the other hand, the tribesmen numbered sixty men—maybe twice that many, depending on how many more had joined the others during the day. What was more, this was their territory, and they were undoubtedly well armed. Finally they'd be fierce fighters, as men always were who had decided they had nothing much left to lose. Nassim was trying to destroy them and had all but succeeded, and as far as they knew they were about to attack just ten Warden Believers.

The sky was cloudy; the night was black. Bolan's orders were that no one was to move but him and his second-in-command, Sokolov. They would move from post to post, finding their way with their night sights. The others were to keep still and scan in all directions.

The warrior took his own position on the crest of the ridge, where he had a good view in all directions. He watched through the sights of his rifle.

Nothing.

For the first hour of the night, nothing. The Masoudi, experienced in this sort of fight, wouldn't move until the people they were going to attack had gone to sleep. The previous night's fiasco had taught them much.

Bolan moved around. He was concerned about Kurt Bittrich. The German swore he felt fit, recovered from the smash on the head. But the Executioner wasn't convinced. He sat apart from the German for a while and studied him through the night sight. Bittrich stayed alert, no question about it.

Looking at Maquala, Bolan saw Raima gently massaging his leg above the boot that was all the cast the man had for his broken ankle.

Jan Huygen was eating, spooning something out of a can, stopping about every thirty seconds to scan his surroundings through his night sight. Ever the professional soldier, he had as much experience at fighting, night and day, as any of them with the possible exception of the Executioner himself; and Bolan imagined he might actually be anticipating the shock of battle with something akin to pleasure.

Anahita Behzad hugged the ground. She scanned the surrounding land through her sight, but she was conspicuously afraid. The woman had courage. She wouldn't be part of the team if she didn't. But she'd had no experience of an actual firefight, particularly in the dark. He could imagine her thoughts and emotions.

The warrior turned to scan their previous positions in the ravine. And through the scope he saw the Masoudi. They scrambled among the places where they'd last seen the combat team in the fading light of the setting sun. He couldn't see the expressions on their faces, but the nervous quality of their movements betrayed their alarm at finding the ravine abandoned. They weren't stupid. They realized they'd been outsmarted, that their prey had moved.

But where?

Suddenly the Masoudi appeared to realize they weren't the hunters anymore; they'd been tricked and stood, perhaps, under the gunsights of their enemies.

The team members had strict orders from their leader. They were not to fire on the Masoudi if the tribesmen retreated.

But they didn't. After their minute of confusion, the Masoudi dropped to the ground and began a slow, cautious advance toward the western slope out of the ravine, toward the ridge line where the combat team was waiting. Their images on the night scopes flickered, green figures moving like so many featureless ghosts.

Bolan couldn't issue any more orders now. The members of the team would fire when they decided they were threatened.

The Masoudi climbed up in what was to them the darkness, their enemy watching like magicians with some kind of unnatural advantage.

A shot rang out. Bolan couldn't tell who had fired and didn't see if one of the Masoudi was hit. But then hell broke loose. The Masoudi pressed forward, confident that the darkness concealed them—and ran straight into the concentrated fire of automatic assault rifles of people they hunted.

Bolan sensed the unfairness of it and couldn't help admiring the fanatic courage of the tribesmen. On the other hand, if he and the team didn't use their advantage, these wild men would overrun them, shoot them or cut their throats.

He saw a man crawling toward him. He'd set the SIG to single shot and fired a round that drilled the crawling greenish figure in the head and stopped him cold. A moment later a grenade exploded.

It was a brief fight. Although the Masoudi couldn't see what was happening, they realized they were taking heavy casualties. In minutes they were retreating and it was over.

In the ensuing silence the warrior checked his teammates. None was hit. He told them, as he moved among them, to be ready to head out in five minutes.

"We have no idea what we've stirred up," he said. "With all that shooting we could get choppers. We've got to put some distance between us and this place—and fast."

Both Sadir and McCulloch supported Maquala, as for the first time they heard him moan. Raima carried his rifle, her father his other gear.

The march in the darkness wasn't easy. After two hours, they'd covered only five miles at most—and they left behind them a trail anyone could follow at first light.

A little before midnight Bolan called a halt. He took the first watch and posted with him the two he most trusted—Jan Huygen and Doug McCulloch. They decided to risk flashing light signals to each other and worked out a simple code—one flash to show their location, two flashes to signal they heard or saw something suspicious, three to signal trouble.

Bolan chose a post on the crest of the ridge. As he sat in the darkness, keeping watch, he began to see distant flares of reddish-orange light—like the flashes of faraway artillery. The flashes continued and became brighter, signaling a thunderstorm in the mountains to the south. In a little while he began to hear it, and he felt the wind beginning to freshen.

The warrior turned and saw Sadir creeping toward him. "It's going to be a fierce storm. This kind of country doesn't see many, but it will be severe. We should find whatever shelter we can."

"Any suggestions?" Bolan asked dryly.

"There is none, of course. But our people must all be on the ridge. The ravine may be flooded."

"Okay. Roust them out."

Wakened from their sleep, the team members scrambled to the top of the ridge and sat staring in fascination and dread at the towering thunderstorm that now swept down from the Ashkab Mountains.

The wind whipped up dust and sand, and they sat with their backs to it, trying to protect their faces. Constantly flashing lightning illuminated the terrain. They were as much exposed as the Masoudi had been.

"No danger of enemies," Sadir commented. "Nobody moves in a storm."

Then the rain hit. It was no more heavy, no more drenching, than rain in any other country, but in this arid place, where they had just climbed out of a desert, the almost solid sheets of wind-driven water were staggering. As Sadir had warned, a rush of water surged through the ravine—not enough to drown anybody perhaps, but enough to sweep away items such as food and medicine. The roar was frightening. The wind tore at clothing, and the rainwater was cold.

After the storm passed, the team sat shivering in their wet clothes, waiting impatiently for the searing heat that would follow a little after sunrise.

"We'll rest and get dry," Bolan told them as they watched the eastern sky begin to lighten. "Until midmorning, anyway."

Dawn broke quickly, and the heat returned. The storm had passed on to the north and the ground dried rapidly. The water in the ravine was rapidly diminishing.

"Chief," McCulloch called softly. He pointed to the northeast. About twenty Masoudi stood on a ridge three-quarters of a mile away, silently staring.

THEY INSISTED he was a CIA agent. He insisted he wasn't. But he didn't know if he'd be any better off if they became convinced he wasn't.

He couldn't guess what they'd do if they found out he wasn't just a CIA station chief as they thought but an NIO, a man with six station chiefs and all their apparatus under his supervision, a man who knew— Well, he knew too damn much.

He had made a bad mistake with his cover story. He'd told them he was a free-lance journalist who wanted to come to Saravabad to interview Hoshab Nassim and to observe his Islamic government in preparation for writing a series of newspaper articles.

Of all the hostages they'd taken off the airplane, he was the only one who had been on his way to Karachistan, to Saravabad. All the rest had been on their way to Pakistan, some as a stopover on their way to Afghanistan or Baluchistan. Of all the passengers on the airliner, he was the only Westerner who had a visa for Karachistan. They had known he was coming. Their consulate in Paris had granted his visa—after much haggling. Maybe that was why they thought he was a spy. After all, why would an American demand and argue for a visa to allow him to travel to a squalid hole like Saravabad?

Besides, he had learned during his captivity that the whole idea of a free-lance journalist was entirely outside the experience and understanding of the Warden

Believers. Their understanding was that newspaper men wrote for their governments, whatever their governments wanted their newspapers to say.

They had beaten him, using brass knuckles, which seemed to be the extent of their sophistication in tough interrogation. His nose was broken, and since it hadn't been set it would remain crooked for the rest of his life probably—though maybe that wasn't going to be long. His left cheekbone was caved in. His right eyebrow was broken in two scabby fragments. He had lost four teeth.

His genitals still ached, although the swelling had gone down some. He'd like to get his hands around the throat of the bastard who had clubbed him between the legs—would like to even the score regardless if it cost him his life.

His chains were a burden but not a torture. They weren't starving him.

Now they were torturing someone else. He could hear them. It was the Sudanese woman. And why, Bob Craig could not imagine.

5

It was impossible to walk across a whole country without running into somebody. Not long after noon their little, spread-out column came across an old man and a boy, shepherding a herd of about thirty or forty sheep on the slope of a hill. The land here was sparsely covered in short, tough grass. Bolan supposed the sheep had a hard time finding enough of it to keep themselves alive. They were, in fact, scrawny animals. The toothless old man and the boy, though, were happy to see ten people they couldn't identify, and they smiled broadly and welcomed them to the hillside.

"I'm not sure," Behzad said, "who they think we are. Wardens, Masoudi... Anyway, they smile because they are afraid of us and want us to think them friends."

"You and Suleiman speak to them," Bolan instructed. "Say something to reassure them. Tell them we are friends."

The white-bearded old man smiled and nodded and seemed to believe whatever it was that Behzad and Zabara said to them. The boy, bolder, walked among the combat team and solemnly observed the modern weapons they carried. He formed his own conclusion obviously, and it was not that these were friendly tourists being guided through Karachistan.

"The old man says there's a Warden station in the valley just over this hill. He says nothing, of course, about the Wardens—only that they are there."

Bolan glanced back to his team. "Anybody spare a couple of cans of fruit?"

Maquala raised his hand and dug into his pack for a can. So did Kurt Bittrich. The German brought forward the two small tins of canned fruit in sugary syrup—one peaches, one pitted cherries. Bolan opened the cans and handed them over.

The boy was delighted and made appreciative sounds as he tipped the can back and swallowed the sweet syrup and chewed on the cherries.

The old shepherd watched the boy skeptically, then tasted the peaches in his can. "Ahh . . ." he muttered.

He turned to the boy and gave him firm orders in the language they spoke. He began also to talk again to Zabara, gesticulating, his eyes wide, his gestures and expressions dramatic.

Behzad listened and translated what the shepherd said for Bolan. "He says the Warden Believers have reinforced their station at the place called Deh Anar. A squad of them arrived yesterday and set out to the north in vehicles."

Then Zabara spoke to Bolan. Again Behzad translated. "He says I am sorry to have to tell you this, my American deliverer, but these evil men have come to this part of Karachistan thinking they might find me and my daughter. They asked this worthy shepherd if he had seen an old man and a woman dressed in man's attire."

"We're a good many miles from where we left your car," Bolan said. "Did they ask about the Masoudi?"

The shepherd's answer was, "Nothing. They are looking for a great traitor, a threat to the very life of Hoshab Nassim." And Behzad added, "I can tell you from the tone of his voice that a threat to the life of Nassim doesn't trouble this man."

The boy returned. He carried a big pitcher and a white ball in a string net.

It was sheep's milk and a ball of sheep milk cheese, the old man's offering to these visitors who had given tins of delicious fruit. Bolan accepted the gifts and the team members ate the impromptu meal.

Deh Anar was on the other side of the hill, the old man said, along the road.

The boy slid up beside Zabara and spoke fast. The man explained to Behzad, and she told Bolan that the boy wanted to go with them to kill Wardens. "He says they are evil men, the enemies of God and man, and he wants his chance to kill some of them."

"Tell him that we aren't going near the Wardens' post. We're going to stay away from it."

She translated, and the boy spit on the ground at Bolan's feet. He turned and walked away, back to the sheep.

"The old man says you must forgive his grandson," Behzad said. "The boy is filled with hatred."

"Tell him I understand."

DEH ANAR WASN'T on the map. The old shepherd, with gestures, had indicated where it would be—on the road, as he emphasized, but the road didn't appear on the map, either.

The shepherd suggested they move in a direction he pointed. It was a little west of south, as Bolan checked his compass. That way, the old man said, they'd stay away from the road and away from the Warden post.

The shepherd had noticed by now that one of their party was hobbling painfully on a broken ankle. He pointed to a green patch on the hill above. There, he said, would be found trees that could be cut to make a litter to carry the injured man.

Bolan thanked him and gave him two more cans of fruit, which the old man received with thanks. Then the team set out again, climbing the hill.

An hour later they reached the small grove of evergreens the shepherd had pointed out. The trees were gnarled and crooked, clinging to life on a barren slope too little watered. The party searched and found, after a while, two trees straight enough to become the poles for a litter. Maquala insisted he could walk, with help, but the trees were cut and the litter constructed.

The Executioner carried the litter the first shift, helped by Bittrich. The German seemed to lack some element of his vision, but he was determined to prove himself. Bolan didn't argue.

The German survived the arduous three-hour shift, over the crest of the hill and starting down, without faltering and without complaint. Bolan began to believe Bittrich had recovered.

There were no signs of the Masoudi. Raima told Behzad the tribesmen believed angry ghosts lived in the hills and mountains, so they wouldn't follow anyone who was so unfair a fighter as to climb up where the ghosts would be their allies.

"That's how they'll explain the night scopes to one another," Behzad said. "The work of hostile spirits."

With Maquala riding on a litter, they could move faster. Bolan wanted to start climbing mountains the next morning.

Brognola had briefed him about getting over the Ashkab Mountains. The range ran in a generally east-west direction. The highest peak, to the west and near the Iranian border, was more than thirteen thousand feet high. A hundred miles to the east of that peak was one that was eleven thousand feet high. Between the two peaks the ridge of the Ashkabs was like the teeth of a giant saw. Crossing anywhere would be a difficult climb, but satellite photos suggested the easiest route might be to the east, near the eleven-thousand-foot peak.

All this showed on his map, and Bolan knew he had to begin working his way east if he was to cross the Ashkabs by this route. He gave McCulloch his binoculars and told the Marine to scout ahead, to climb higher and look out for the Warden station the shepherd had warned them about. Once he was sure they'd passed that hazard, they'd turn east.

Working their way southward, they saw goats but no goatherds. They had climbed high enough already that they could look back over the desert they had crossed.

Bolan called a halt and said they'd take half an hour to rest and eat. He went to check Maquala. The young Arab was in pain but doggedly cheerful. He was also thankful to the men who were carrying him on the litter.

Zabara and Behzad smoked. It was difficult for them to be without their harsh Turkish cigarettes. They sat cross-legged and puffed away, chatting quietly in Urdu while Raima wandered a few yards away to relieve herself.

McCulloch hadn't yet returned from scouting, and Bolan was concerned about how long the Marine had been gone. He scanned the ridges and slopes ahead but caught no sight of the man.

Behzad rose and hurried off in the direction Raima had taken. She reappeared a moment later. "Striker! Raima's gone! She wouldn't leave us. Something's happened to her."

Two missing—Doug McCulloch and now Raima. Bolan split the rest of the team into two groups—half taking shelter among the rocks in the basin where they'd stopped to rest, the other half forming a patrol to circle the camp. Sokolov commanded the camp defense, Bolan the patrol. Bittrich and Behzad stayed with Sokolov, as did Maquala and Zabara. Bolan led Huygen and Sadir out to recon the area.

Half an hour later Bolan and his patrol returned. They'd seen nothing of Raima or McCulloch.

"We've got no choice but to move on," Bolan said grimly. He turned to Behzad. "Tell Zabara I'd go looking for her if I had the least idea where to look."

Behzad nodded and translated for the girl's father.

THE TEAM MADE its way higher into the foothills. Bolan took the point. Two of his people were missing, and it was obvious that someone was watching them, someone who wasn't far away. When one of them left the protection of the group, he or she was fair game.

A pebble dropped at his feet. He swung the muzzle of his SIG 550 toward the direction he thought the little rock had come from.

"Chief!"

He lowered the muzzle at the sound of McCulloch's voice.

"They've got Raima!" McCulloch announced when he scrambled down the slope. "I saw them hustling her off."

"Who?"

"Well, not the Masoudi. These guys had uniforms. Got to be Warden Believers. Four of them. They had her! They were between me and you, and I couldn't get back to tell you. Mean-lookin' mothers. Got Uzis."

"Where were they going with her when you saw them?"

McCulloch pointed east.

"Deh Anar," Bolan muttered. "The Warden station on the road."

"Chief, she knows a hell of a lot."

THE EXECUTIONER LAY on the rocky ground and watched the Warden station through his binoculars. It was a concrete block building, squat and square. Two small military vehicles were parked at the side.

"There's no electricity and no radio antennae," Bolan said to McCulloch and Huygen, the two men he'd chosen to accompany him.

"There are radios in those jeeps," McCulloch stated.

Bolan nodded. "To talk to each other, talk to choppers, talk back here to headquarters if they're not more than twenty, thirty miles out. Those radios aren't talking to Saravabad."

"Don't you think it's possible Raima is still there?" Huygen asked.

Bolan shrugged. "Hauled off in a chopper maybe..."

"No chopper," McCulloch replied. "I was up above this place. I didn't see a chopper, or hear one."

"So if they brought her here, she's in there," Huygen said.

"Sure. Where else?" McCulloch asked.

"On the road to Saravabad," Bolan said.

"Well, I suppose we've got to find out."

"Right," Bolan agreed. "And the sooner the better."

"We can't wait for dark," Huygen told them solemnly.

They had to do a close recon on the Warden station in broad daylight, and one thing was in their favor. Whoever built the station had known nothing about military architecture. Maybe he knew something about keeping the heat of the sun out of buildings, but he knew nothing about giving the men inside fields of view—or fields of fire, for that matter—out all sides of the building. It sat in a curve in the road, where its front faced north. That side was out of sight to Bolan but probably contained the doors and windows, which were away from direct sunlight. There was a back door, where apparently the men walked out to relieve themselves on the ground, but that door had no window. The roof extended well out beyond the eaves to keep sunlight off the walls.

What was an advantage was also a disadvantage. The team could get no idea of how many men were in the building—or whether Raima was there—except by looking in from the front. And that meant looking in from the road.

"All right," Bolan said. "I want you to stay up here, Doug. Watch out for patrols and warn us if you can. Let them have it if you've got no choice." He handed McCulloch the binoculars, and the Marine dropped to his belly between two rocks and set himself to watch.

Bolan and Huygen began to work their way down the slope toward the concrete block building. They were exposed. In addition to rocks there was a sparse vegetation on the slope, a tough kind of grass and some light green weeds. But there was no cover.

The two combat-suited soldiers continued on until they were within fifty yards of the rear of the Warden station. They stopped to watch and listen for a minute, then started down again.

Bolan pointed to the left. Huygen nodded and moved away from him. The Executioner headed to the right.

A minute later they were at the rear of the building. Huygen slipped around the corner and checked the west side. Bolan checked the east. They went back to the rear to signal the all-clear.

It was then that the door opened and a Warden Believer stepped outside. He was a big man, wearing a red beret and khaki shirt and pants, all stained with sweat. He wore the copper bracelet Behzad had pointed out on the bodies of the Wardens killed by the Masoudi, and in a holster on his right hip he carried what looked like a Tokarev automatic.

Because of the way the door swung, he saw Bolan first; and because he saw Bolan and his attention was focused on the warrior, he didn't see Jan Huygen. He scrambled for his pistol, but before he could draw it Huygen's throwing knife hit between his shoulder blades and plunged in six inches. He threw both hands behind his back, clawing for the knife. While he struggled Huygen pounced and slashed his bayonet across the man's throat.

Bolan chanced a look inside the door but couldn't see anyone. The rear door of the station opened into what was apparently a storage room.

Huygen dragged the body around the corner of the building. Then the two soldiers knelt outside the door and talked.

"One of us could go in," Huygen suggested, nodding at the door, "and—"

A rock clattered down the slope. They looked up to see McCulloch on his knees and pointing at the road to the east.

Peering out from behind the Warden station, Bolan and Huygen spotted an approaching car. It was a battered old sedan, of Russian manufacture from the look of it, painted a sickly light green. A dark green flag flew from the left front fender. As the vehicle neared the station, the driver gave a blast on a siren. The sedan drew up in front of the building in a cloud of dust.

"I'd say that car's here to take Raima to Saravabad," Bolan said.

"That would be my guess, too."

"Can't let it happen. First thing's to try to take out the vehicle. Cover me."

Bolan moved around the side of the station to where the two military vehicles were parked. He trotted over to the first one and crouched in the cover it provided against a view from the road. He waited, and no one reacted. He glanced back at Huygen, who nodded.

The Executioner slashed the tires on one side of the vehicle with his bayonet, then crawled to the second vehicle and repeated the procedure. Huygen moved forward and took up his covering position between the two vehicles. The green sedan was parked on the road, its rear extending beyond the east wall of the station. Crawling between the wall and the second of the two jeeps, Bolan came within six feet of the left rear tire of the car. But as he took a quick, cautious look around the corner, he saw that two Wardens stood near the front of the vehicle.

He looked back at Huygen. The two soldiers could signal a good many things without words, and Huygen quickly understood what the problem was. He gestured to Bolan to hang in while he went around the building the other way and tried something.

Bolan nodded his understanding with a cautioning sign and crouched to wait for whatever Huygen had planned. While he waited, he fixed his bayonet to the SIG 550. He had an idea how he'd use it.

On the west side of the building Huygen pulled the pin from a grenade, counted down, then lobbed the bomb as far as his muscular arm could throw it. The grenade sailed across the road and down the slope on the far side, where it exploded with a sound like thunder.

A trio of Wardens ran out of the building, firing their AK-47s wildly into the smoke and dust roiling up the gully beyond the road. The two Wardens who had been standing near the front of the car raced across and joined them, firing with pistols. Bolan slid forward and jammed his bayonet into the tire.

The Wardens stopped shooting but continued to shout. Neither Bolan nor Huygen could understand a word they said, but it made no difference. The voices gave the two soldiers a better idea of how many men were in the station. Six or seven probably, and there were five outside. The odds weren't good.

A Warden stalked around the rear of the green sedan and opened the door on the far side. Then a door slammed out of sight to Bolan and Huygen, hiding between the two little vehicles and the wall.

More yelling. The sedan's engine kicked to life. The driver jammed it into gear and stepped on the accelerator. The station building blocked their view of what happened next, but Bolan and Huygen could hear. The flattened left rear tire flapped and shredded, and the sedan stopped.

"It's in the fan," Bolan whispered. "Time to back off a little."

He had judged right. Two Wardens ran around the end of the building to the jeeps. Bolan and Huygen had just slipped around to the rear of the building.

Suddenly they heard the harsh rip of automatic rifle fire. Bolan jerked his head around in time to see two Wardens stumble from the rear door of the station and fall, gut shot by a deadly burst.

He glanced up the slope just long enough to see McCulloch pull his SIG 550 back into the cover of his hiding place. The bipod was extended on the rifle and had given the big Marine the accuracy of fire that had taken down the two Wardens. He had seen them coming and had taken them out.

Now it was really in the fan.

"I only see one way for this," Bolan told his companion. "In the back door. Inside. Maybe the only place where they're not gunning for us."

Huygen nodded and trotted toward the door. He set himself to fire a burst into the building, saw no one and charged inside, followed by Bolan.

As they had thought, the back room was a storeroom stacked with cartons and boxes. Another door led into the station proper.

Huygen provided cover and Bolan gave the door a kick. Two men stood inside the spare, shabby room that was the station office. They were staring out the front door, but they spun, raising the muzzles of their Uzis. Bolan took them with a short burst.

The broad front window of the station dissolved in an explosion of glass as one or more Wardens realized the enemy was inside and fired a burst at the window. Bolan and Huygen had anticipated the move and had kept out of the line of fire. Now they stepped over to the frame and fired bursts through the opening.

A woman shrieked in terror, and Bolan knew it had to be Raima. He risked a look through the shattered window. Yeah. She was in the rear seat of the green sedan, held down by two men.

Bolan let loose a burst at the hood of the car. He had no intentions of letting them drive away with her.

Huygen rushed to the window on the east side of the station, looking out on the two jeeps. He took one man down with a burst, then fired into the radios of the two vehicles.

"Striker," he said as he turned to Bolan, "I think we're better than even now."

"A lot better," the Executioner agreed.

But not yet. McCulloch suddenly opened fire from his position on the slope above the station.

Bolan looked through the window and spotted what McCulloch was firing on—an incoming Warden patrol. They had been six, but McCulloch had cut them down to four. Now they were working their way in carefully, each man running in a crouch, dashing from one rock to another.

McCulloch picked off another one. The others ran past him, mostly interested now in reaching the cover of the station.

Bolan fired a burst that took down two more. The last man turned and ran. McCulloch got him.

The warrior stepped out the front door of the Warden station. Two men sat in the rear seat of the sedan, with Raima between them. The driver sat in front.

The two men in the back seat wore the khaki uniform of the Warden Believers, with the copper ID bracelets, but with military caps, not berets. The man on the right side held a pistol to Raima's head.

The Warden officers stared hard at Bolan and Huygen. The one on the left drew a pistol and placed the muzzle to Raima's face.

"Stalemate," Huygen said.

McCulloch crept forward, his boots silent on the gravel. He stood for a moment, staring at the sedan and the terrified Raima between the two Wardens. Then he walked to the sedan, thrust the muzzle of his SIG 550 through the open window and aimed it straight at the left-hand officer's crotch.

"You don't speak English maybe, but I figure you get my meaning." He showed the Warden officer a broad grin. "Don't you?"

The officer glanced at the other officer, then put his pistol down. The other officer did the same.

"See?" McCulloch said. "There are ways of educating anybody."

Bolan walked around to the right side of the sedan, meaning to open the door and pull one of the officers out. But suddenly three pistol shots rang out.

Raima had shot each of the officers in the head, then the driver through the back of the seat. Bolan opened the door, and the dead officer tumbled out into the dust of the road.

6

Bolan led the team southeast and onto ever higher ground, the heat abating slightly. They found mountain ponds where streams of snow melt trickled down from above and they could fill their canteens again.

The Executioner spread them wide over the face of the slope they were climbing. They could be seen from below, and he figured that a man with binoculars would be less likely to see a ragged horizontal line than a column climbing together.

For a few minutes Raima and her father walked beside Bolan, with Behzad to translate. "They were taking me back to Hoshab Nassim," the woman said through Behzad. "They wanted to know who you were and why I was with you. I didn't tell them."

"How long had they been following us?" Bolan asked.

"I don't know. Their orders were to look for me and my father. Every Warden Believer station in Karachistan is under orders to find us."

"When they find the station with its squad wiped out, they'll know a foreign force has landed in Karachistan," Bolan stated.

Behzad translated this, and Zabara shook his head and spoke at some length. She interpreted for Bolan.

"He says what you suggest isn't necessarily true. He says that he, Suleiman Zabara, was and is a man of position and influence in Karachistan. He says he has many friends who hate Nassim and that the Warden Believers may think a dissident force has arisen. Raima, he says, is a...well, the closest word might be 'princess.' As a wife of Nassim, she, too, has special status. The government may think it faces a revolution."

Zabara continued and Behzad translated. "He says he's ashamed that all he was doing when we found him was trying to flee the country. But he knew Nassim would put Raima to death by torture if his men caught her. He was determined to get her out of the country before he tried to lead an attack."

"Tell him that we're here to free some hostages, not to overthrow the government. As soon as we accomplish what we came here for, we'll be leaving. Tell him to think about whether he wants to come with us when we leave."

Zabara heard the translation and bobbed toward Bolan in a little bow.

"And tell the princess," Bolan added, "that killing three men after we've taken them prisoner isn't our way of doing things. If for no better reason, she should have understood that I might have wanted to interrogate them."

CLIMBING BECAME more difficult. It wasn't any longer just a matter of trudging wearily upward. The team had to look for ways around steep rock faces and ways to cross deep ravines.

Bolan wanted to put as much distance as possible between his group and the Warden station before they stopped for the night. But he had to consider how long a day it had been and how tired his team was getting. It would be a mistake to exhaust them. He decided he'd call a halt before sunset. When they came upon a small grove a gnarled mountain pines, the warrior decided this was as good a place as any.

As the team struck camp, Maquala called Bolan to his side. "This would be a good place for me to stay. You can leave me food. There is water near enough so that I can get to it. When you have completed the mission, you can send a chopper to pick me up here."

Bolan shook his head. "That would leave me short a man. I might need you to guard the princess."

"Princess?"

"Raima."

Bolan stood and walked away, knowing that Raima was capable of guarding herself and wouldn't need a bodyguard. She and her father were armed now. She'd taken the Tokarev pistols from the bodies of the Warden officers she'd killed, then had searched their pockets and the car for more ammo. The Executioner had no doubt of what she'd do if somebody tried to kidnap her again.

He sat down beside Jan Huygen, who was eating his evening meal. "What about Ali?"

Huygen shook his head. "He's not going to get any better. More likely he'll get worse."

"He wants to stay behind until we can send someone for him."

"Better not." Huygen pointed down the mountainside. The road, the only one in this region, was five miles behind and below them, but they could see the headlights of a convoy of vehicles stabbing through the darkness.

Bolan lifted his binoculars. "Trucks," he pronounced.

"Not a coincidence," Huygen stated matter-of-factly.

IN THE FIRST LIGHT OF DAWN Bolan saw the trucks parked along the road. Men were tending cooking fires, preparing breakfast.

Behzad, too, studied them through Bolan's binoculars. "Cobras," she said, "not Wardens. It doesn't make much difference. The Karachistan Cobra Force is just as loyal to Nassim as the Warden Believers. And they're tougher, too—better disciplined, better armed."

Suleiman Zabara approached and spoke to Behzad. "He wants to tell you something," she said.

"Go ahead."

Zabara spoke and Behzad translated. "He says there's a mountain village about sixteen kilometers west of here. He can show it to you on the map. The doctor there has a little clinic. If you could somehow manage to get Ali there, the doctor could set his ankle."

Bolan made a decision. Ten minutes later he carried the front of the litter and Sadir the rear. The doctor, Zabara had told Bolan, didn't know him but might have heard of him. He was willing to go to the village to help. Sadir spoke enough Urdu to understand and make himself understood, although haltingly. Behzad had wanted to go, too, but Bolan said the rest of the team would need her as guide and translator. Besides, Sadir could carry his end of the litter, and she couldn't. Sokolov would lead the rest of the team.

Bolan and the Russian compared maps. Sokolov would lead his party of six eastward up the mountain.

If Bolan and his group didn't catch up with them by noon the next day, they'd strike camp and wait overnight. If Bolan didn't rendezvous by morning, the six would continue on to Saravabad.

Zabara had said the village was sixteen kilometers distant, and the warrior meant to cover that distance in two hours—or not much more. Sadir was strong enough to do it. Zabara strode along and didn't complain.

There was risk that the Cobras on the road below might spot them, but not much. Even with good binoculars, at five miles an observer had little chance of picking out a small party on the vast side of a mountain.

So they made good time. By the end of the two hours they could see the village ahead—a dusty mountain settlement built of dun-colored brick, sleeping lazily in the morning sun.

"Most of the men and boys will be out tending sheep," Sadir told them. "The women will be in the surrounding fields, where they try to grow a little grain, a few vegetables."

Zabara spoke and Sadir translated. "He says he should go into the village alone. The appearance of men in combat clothes will alarm the people. He can find the doctor and assure everyone we aren't hostile."

Bolan frowned. "Okay. Tell him to go ahead."

Zabara headed toward the village, at first half walking, half trotting; and then, when perhaps he thought someone in the village had noticed him, he straightened his shoulders and walked with great dignity.

"Do you trust him?" Bolan asked Sadir.

"Yes, I do."

"Okay. But let's move. I want to be under cover, with a good field of fire in front of me, when somebody comes out of that village."

They picked up Maquala and carried him a hundred yards downhill, where they stopped behind a slight rise in the land. A few minutes later Zabara walked out of the village, accompanied by a tall, white-bearded man wearing a white robe and turban.

Bolan rose and beckoned the two men. The white-robed man knelt beside Maquala and frowned over his boot.

Zabara spoke, and Sadir told Bolan the old man's name was Dr. Shiraz.

With impatient professional skill the doctor used a sharp knife to cut away the boot, exposing the swollen flesh of the ankle. He turned down the corners of his mouth and grumbled.

"He says, 'bad,'" Sadir explained. "He says 'death.'"

"Death?"

"I know not the word, Striker. If I understand what he says, he speaks of what in English you call gangrene."

Zabara began to talk. Sadir stopped him with a frantic gesture, and for a minute or two they talked with their hands as well as their mouths until Sadir nodded and seemed to understand.

"Zabara says the village hates Hoshab Nassim, a heretic and renegade. He says there isn't a man in the village who would betray Ali's presence to the Warden Believers."

Bolan knelt beside the young man. "Do you understand what's being said?"

Maquala nodded, a fearful expression on his face.

The doctor was talking again, and Sadir translated. "He says, who will know this young man is not a shepherd injured in a fall on the mountainside?"

"In any village," Bolan said, "there are traitors."

Dr. Shiraz heard the translation, then stood and stared hard at Bolan. He spoke angrily.

"The doctor says that such traitors have long since been buried a kilometer from the village, that the stench of their corpses may not befoul the air."

"Tell the doctor I'll return for this man. Keep him well."

The doctor listened to Sadir, nodded gravely, then spoke.

"He says honor is the shared property of all good men. He says he supposes your word is good. Well, so is his. Ali will be looked after as if he were his own son."

BOLAN LED SADIR and Zabara east again and up toward the crest of the mountain ridge and the rendezvous point where he hoped to find Sokolov and the rest of the team. Zabara proudly carried the SIG 550 that had been Maquala's, and as they walked Sadir explained to him how it operated.

They had achieved what they had hoped to achieve. Maquala would be taken care of. They had made good time. By nightfall they should be over the crest of the mountain, and by noon they should rejoin the main party.

Bolan called a halt when they had neared the point where they had separated from the others four hours ago. They sat down to rest, and he used his binoculars to examine the long mountain slopes beneath them, down to the road where the convoy of trucks had unloaded a company or more of what were probably Karachistan Cobra Force detachments.

The trucks were still there, sitting in line on the road. The Cobras were nowhere to be seen.

Bolan had no doubt of what was going on. The enemy was searching the whole region within miles of where they had found the shattered Warden station.

An attack in sufficient force to do that meant rebellion, if indeed it didn't mean invasion. The Masoudi didn't knock out whole stations—they didn't have the firepower to accomplish that.

But squads of men working the mountainside were no more visible than were the men and women of Bolan's team. On the long, wide landscape of the mountain binocular scans sighted people only with good luck.

They ate and drank a little, then moved on. The mountains now dominated everything. They loomed above, the wind blowing plumes of snow off their peaks. To attempt a climb of those steep, rocky peaks, with deep crevices hidden by snow, where sheer, almost vertical cliffs rose hundreds of feet, was too much of a challenge for men and women not specially equipped for it. Sokolov was following the course Bolan had given him: eastward to the streams and pass that cut through the mountain chain.

Sokolov and the main party were four hours closer. Bolan hoped they reached the pass and crossed through before nightfall.

Zabara spoke to Sadir. "The man has sharp eyes. He thinks he sees a patrol."

The old man rose on his knees, squinted and pointed at what he saw. He was right. Bolan spotted a patrol of ten or twelve men on the mountainside below, about a mile away, moving toward their position.

"I don't want to get into a firefight now," Bolan said. "The noise would attract the whole company. We've got to get to cover."

Sadir translated for Zabara, and the three men crawled toward a shallow defile, which was the only cover they had any chance of reaching without being seen.

Their cover was anything but adequate. The first Cobra who stared hard in their direction would see them.

The patrol kept plodding upward. Bolan studied the men through his binoculars. This troop was well armed and well disciplined. They wore camouflage fatigues and helmets and carried assault rifles. On their sleeves was the distinctive insignia of Cobra Force—a black snake sewed to the uniform and encircling the arm. They were obviously tired. They'd been climbing all morning, while the Executioner and his party had been mostly walking a horizontal course along the slope of the mountain to the village and back. They trudged onward, keeping their heads down.

If they continued on their present course, they would walk within fifty yards of where Bolan and his companions crouched.

The beating of rotors signaled the arrival of a chopper. It flew east to west and was coming fast. There was no hiding from it.

The chopper slowed, then stopped, hovering. Bolan could do nothing but stare, waiting for somebody in the aircraft to see him and open fire.

One of the men in the patrol—its commanding officer most likely—stepped a little apart from the others. He pulled out the antenna on a Handie-Talkie and began to talk, obviously to the helicopter pilot.

For several minutes the aircraft hovered above the patrol while the officer talked on the radio. Then the chopper rose and swept away to the west. The patrol continued on up the mountain.

"Somebody up there's looking out for us," Bolan said to Sadir when they were together again. "The guys in the chopper and the Cobras were so interested in each other that no one looked in this direction. Relax while you can. We'll let that patrol put another half hour's distance between it and us before we move out."

SAUDA WRITHED and grunted under the blast of cold water from the nozzle of a big canvas hose. Her captors had taken off the blindfold but had left the painful wooden bit in place. Her arms were still chained, as were her legs. She remained naked.

One of the two men yelled something harsh at the other. The second man frowned, then turned the nozzle to scatter the water into a spray.

This was better. It stung but didn't bruise, although when he shot the spray on her face, she thought she'd drown.

She understood now what they were doing. This was a bath. And they kept it up until she shivered from the cold.

With a curt gesture the man with the hose ordered her to her feet. She scrambled up and stood staring at him, trembling.

He stepped around behind her and unlocked the handcuffs that had held her arms rigidly behind her back for... She'd lost count of the days.

It wasn't release from agony. Her shoulders seemed locked; the cramped joints resisted movement. Only very slowly and very painfully could she bring her hands down to her sides and then cautiously around.

At the same time he released the bit from her mouth. She shoved it with her tongue and it fell to the floor. Then Sauda began to cry.

When she regained her composure, she was given a white robe to wear and was led out into a courtyard. When she saw the wall, the stake and the firing squad, her knees buckled. She realized she was to be shot.

The men who escorted her held her up, but they didn't lead her to the stake. Instead, they took her to another wall to one side of the courtyard.

Because her eyes had been fastened on the firing squad and the stake, she hadn't noticed that half a dozen other people stood to one side, the other hostages—but not Ibrahim, her husband.

It happened in less than a minute. They led Ibrahim Sadik quickly to the stake. He was already bound. They looped a heavy belt around him and buckled it behind, fastening him to the stake. The men stepped back to a safe distance, the officer gave one sharp command and a volley from five rifles blasted Sadik's blood and flesh against the wall behind the stake.

Sauda Sadik—or maybe now she was Melanie Helms again—screamed and collapsed to the ground. Before she lost consciousness she focused on a window in the main building of the villa and saw a face. It was Hoshab Nassim, calmly nibbling on some tidbit of food as he watched the execution.

THEY FED HER. Her mouth was so sore from wearing the wooden bit that she could hardly chew, and eating was a slow process. Then they led her to a tub and told her to bathe with soap.

Afterward they presented her with another white robe, modest headdress and sandals. She was in the main building of the villa, one of the palaces of Nassim's. She stayed away from the windows of the room—out of fear that if she looked from a window she might see the wall stained with the blood of her husband.

An elderly man came to speak to her. "In the name of God, the beneficent, the merciful . . . Our most esteemed and dearly beloved great leader has, of his boundless wisdom and kindness, elected to extend to you the honor of his tent. Blessed is the name of God. Blessed is the name of his Prophet. Blessed is the name of his servant Hoshab Nassim."

Sauda was staggered. "The honor of his tent . . ." The man who had just ordered the murder of her husband was now summoning her to sleep with him.

7

In the last light of the setting sun Bolan and his companions reached a mountain pass that had to be the one on Brognola's satellite photo. It was as it had been described—a shallow valley where a small river flowed north through the mountains. South of the mountains the river was dry now, but in the valley where it cut through the chain, it was fed by snowmelt rushing down from the mountaintops in rivulets.

A pass through the mountains. Also a trap. Wardens or Cobras could move fast along the road. He knew he wouldn't risk his two men down there, and he was confident Sokolov hadn't. They could use the pass to reach the south side of the Ashkab Mountains—but only by travelling along the side of the pass above the river and road, not by going down to where the going would be easy.

He looked for a place where they could spend the night and found a sandy basin where a tangle of low evergreens afforded some cover. As they settled down, they heard the sound of engines and looked down to see two trucks speeding north along the road beside the river. The plume of dust from those two vehicles had hardly settled before a motorcycle rushed by. Sadir volunteered for first watch.

When he woke Bolan, a crescent moon hung low over the mountains. The team had intentionally parachuted into Karachistan in the dark phase of the moon. As far as Bolan was concerned, the moon could stay dark for another week. But it wouldn't, and the mission could be more dangerous because of the moonlight.

Sadir had reported that his watch had been uneventful, other than occasional traffic on the road across the river. As Bolan assumed his vantage point, he saw a motorcycle speeding south, then a small car heading north. He was more concerned about boots scraping on gravel, or voices. Vehicles traveling quickly on the road were no threat.

It was a quiet watch until the moon provided enough light to cast shadows. Then, looking down at the river on the near side, the Executioner spotted three men, moving north, keeping close to the water's edge. They seemed to be hurrying, yet were furtive.

Because of the trees that grew along the river, Bolan couldn't at first make any kind of identification. Then the trio moved out into the open space between two sparse stands of small trees, and he got a good look at them.

Two of them were Warden Believers. They wore khaki uniforms with red berets and carried short automatic weapons. The men kept looking behind them, and across the river, as if they wanted to be sure that their movements were undetected.

The third man, now that Bolan got a good look at him, was their prisoner. His hands were tied or cuffed behind his back, and he was having difficulty maintaining his balance and keeping up with his captors.

The three men were a little south of Bolan's position, but soon they would pass within ten yards of him. The warrior roused Sadir, put a finger to his mouth to signal for silence, then pointed at the approaching men. Sadir squinted into the gloomy light of dawn and nodded. Bolan pointed to Suleiman Zabara, who was sleeping soundly, and signaled Sadir to let him be.

The Executioner left the cover of the little depression where they'd spent the night and worked his way down toward the water. He wasn't sure whether he wanted to interfere with these two Warden Believers and their prisoner, but he might when he got a better idea who the prisoner was. He moved closer to their path to have a closer look and be ready.

The prisoner lost his balance and fell. The two Wardens jerked him up, and one landed a punch on his jaw.

"Take it easy!" the prisoner mumbled in English.

American? It was hard to tell. But hearing English from the man prompted Bolan to get involved. This was no ordinary Karachistani citizen who'd committed a crime. The Executioner's interest was piqued.

Bolan inched forward among the trees and rocks, a little closer to where they would pass, intending to get a better look at the prisoner. From its scabbard on his belt the warrior withdrew his Bali-Song, the lethal Philippine knife he'd used on more than one occasion. In a quick, practiced motion he unfolded the handles, exposing the blade. The two handles were made of steel and could be gripped together in one hand or could be spread apart like wings to give a man two-handed power in driving the blade home. He shoved the handles together and gripped the knife in his right hand.

With his left he picked up a rock, and when the trio was almost upon him, he tossed it a few yards ahead of them. It landed with a clatter.

The Warden Believers froze and peered ahead, conspicuously spooked. One of them took a few cautious steps forward, his Uzi up and ready. The other dropped into a crouch.

Bolan lunged forward and pounded the blade into the Warden's throat, a deadly stab that silenced the man instantly. He didn't let the Warden fall, merely wrestled him gently into a small tree and left him propped up. With a bit of luck his comrade would think he was alive.

The prisoner gaped with shock and confusion. Bolan signaled him to keep silent and backed off a pace into his cover.

The other Warden shrugged, deciding he'd heard nothing alarming. He returned the few paces to where the prisoner stood openmouthed, gawking.

The Warden said something harsh to the dead man—which were his last words. The six-inch blade of the Bali-Song slipped between two ribs in his back and punctured his heart. The knife was withdrawn, then plunged in again. The man dropped to his knees, then fell forward.

The warrior turned to the prisoner. "I think I heard you speak English."

"I guess you did," the man replied. "Who in the name of God are you? I mean, thanks, fella. I was on my way to something worse than death. But—"

"American?"

"Yeah. Gib Barnes. Uh, the key to these cuffs is in the pocket of the one you took out first."

Bolan squatted beside the man and began to go through his pockets. He took the time to have a closer look at Barnes. He was a big fellow, about fifty years old, with white hair, ruddy cheeks—a broad-shouldered, athletic-looking sort of man. He was dressed in sturdy hiking boots, khaki pants, a blue checkered wool shirt and a dark blue jacket.

"Oh-oh!" Barnes muttered.

He had looked up to see Ardeshir Sadir arrive from up the slope.

"Friend of mine," Bolan said. "You want to tell us who you are?"

"As a matter of fact, I sort of have to trade that info with you. You see, I'm not supposed to be here."

"Neither are we," Bolan said dryly.

He hadn't yet found the key, and he gestured to Sadir to go through the pockets of the other body.

"Unofficial," Barnes mused. "Well, so am I. Let's not be too demanding of each other, hmm? Seeing a combat-equipped American in the Ashkab Mountains, I'll guess your being here has something to do with the hostages in Saravabad."

"I've heard about those hostages," Bolan admitted.

"Yes, well, so have I. Heard about them. Good enough. And your interest is, uh..."

"One of them is an American. One of the eight."

Barnes shook his head. "Two of the seven."

"Come again."

"There are only seven left. They shot one yesterday."

"Two Americans?"

"One isn't supposed to be, but is."

"You're better informed than I am," Bolan told the man. He had found the key and now unlocked Barnes's handcuffs. "Are you going to tell me where you get it?"

"I was in Saravabad yesterday. To be frank with you, I'd given up on my job. The one they shot yesterday was the one I was interested in. I had all the necessary papers for coming into Karachistan legally, including a permit to drive a car. Officially I was supposed to be in the country to open another one of their always futile searches for oil."

"There's no oil in Karachistan," Sadir said.

"Not a drop," Barnes agreed. "But try telling that to Nassim. He just can't believe God would have blessed the heretical Iranians with oil and not the true-believing Karachistanis. I think he suspects there's a conspiracy of geologists. Anyway, I was supposed to be looking at rock formations."

"What were you doing here really?" Bolan asked.

"Working for a living," Barnes said. "I took a job. I was supposed to see what I could do about getting a man out of Saravabad. Yesterday they shot him."

"One of the hostages."

"Yes. Ibrahim Sadik. A Sudanese. Please don't ask who was paying me."

"So what were you doing with Warden Believers?" Bolan asked.

Barnes bent over one of the dead men and picked up his Uzi. By the way he checked it over, Bolan could tell the man had handled a machine pistol before. He took the extra magazines from the man's kit, then looked up at Bolan and grinned. "With your permission..."

The warrior shrugged. "What was the idea?" he asked, nodding at the two Wardens.

"I had a Land Rover and enough gas to get to the Afghan border. I was trying to make an overnight drive. These two beauties stopped me about five miles south of here. A couple of Cobras came along, too, and they commandeered the Land Rover to go back to Saravabad. They ordered the two Wardens to march me up the road to the first station. But this pair talked it over and decided I was worth money. They were taking me to a village where they were going to hide me until they could find out what I was worth."

Bolan decided to accept that. He didn't believe every word, but he knew he wasn't going to get any more out of the man.

"Are you going to tell me any more about yourself?" Barnes asked.

"Not really. Call me Striker. I'm going south."

"To Saravabad?"

"That's possible."

"Two of you?"

"There are others."

Barnes raised his chin and for a moment stared skeptically at Bolan, then at Sadir. "Assault rifles, grenades. I'd guess you're part of a combat team."

"Don't guess too much," Bolan warned.

Barnes glanced around. "Can you use another man? I've soldiered some. I can carry my weight. Speak the language a little."

"A mercenary," Bolan stated.

"I've been called worse."

"You come with me, you take orders," Bolan said. "Absolutely and all the time. You might not like the mission, but once you come with us you're a part of it. To the end."

Barnes nodded. "Understood. You the top soldier in this outfit?"

"I'm in command. There's a second-in-command. You take his orders, too."

"I've got no other way to get out of Karachistan alive. You want to hide these bodies?"

TRAVELING NEAR THE ROAD and the river was dangerous in daylight. Bolan led his group up the mountainside and put a mile between them and the bottom of the pass. They scrambled along a rocky slope, following the pass south.

They had until noon to catch up with Sokolov and the main party, and the warrior pressed them hard, not knowing what they might encounter that would slow their progress before they reached their rendezvous point. Barnes didn't complain, even though he was as old as Zabara and probably not in condition to make a long, hard march.

He had enough breath to talk, and he told Bolan he suspected one of the hostages was a plant, a traitor to the group. "I mean, Nassim had no idea I was in town to try to rescue Ibrahim Sadik. He didn't have him shot because he found out about me. He had him shot because he found out— Well, the people who hired me to try to get the guy out had their reasons. Nassim found out about them."

"I think it's time you told me those reasons," Bolan said.

"I can tell you this much. Sadik was an intelligence agent."

"Whose?"

"I'd appreciate it if you didn't press that point. Not for his own government, I can tell you that. The government involved was paying me a lot of money to— Well, to be frank, I was to get him out, or kill him if I had to. He knew too much."

"Then maybe somebody else working for the same government . . ."

"No, he wasn't killed by the government that hired me. He was shot on the orders of Nassim by a firing squad."

"If Nassim knew he was a spy, why would he shoot him?" Bolan asked. "The guy could have passed on a lot of information."

"Nassim didn't know who he had," Barnes stated. "Somebody laid some kind of accusation on Sadik, something that would motivate Nassim to have him shot. But you're right. It wasn't an accusation that Sadik was an intelligence agent."

"Was Sadik working for the U.S. government?"

Barnes shook his head emphatically. "Absolutely not. And neither am I."

THEY HAD TO STOP from time to time and take cover when they spotted vehicles and patrols on the road in the valley below. A convoy of twenty trucks moved north, accompanied by six armored cars. The unpaved road, Barnes explained, was the main route from Saravabad and the coastal towns of Karachistan to the deserts and mountains of the northwest.

Bolan kept a close eye behind them and above. He had to wonder what had happened to the patrols they'd seen on the mountain the previous day. If they were above, watching with binoculars, they would see his group and could use their radios to call in attack helicopters.

At least once an hour one or two choppers flew through the mountain pass, keeping a few hundred feet above the river and road. They passed close to the four men on the mountainside, but they moved fast and didn't seem to be looking for anyone in the pass.

"We're looking at a hell of a lot more than normal military traffic," commented Barnes. "Have you guys stirred up something?"

"I wouldn't be surprised if the Warden Believers have a grudge against us," Bolan said.

"Well, they're moving north, and we're going south."

An hour before noon they reached the rendezvous point. They approached cautiously, Bolan out in front, scanning the area, looking for the rest of the team. He saw no one and was concerned. The patrol he had managed to avoid the previous afternoon had moved southeast and could have caught up with Sokolov and the others. A patrol of twenty men, part of a company of a hundred...supported by choppers.

The rendezvous point wasn't a "point." It was actually an area half a mile square that he and the Russian had been able to identify on the map by its proximity to a sharp mountain ridge and by its bearing from a village ten miles or so below on the south slope of the Ashkab Mountains.

This was the ridge, and Bolan could see the village. Through his binoculars he could identify the village as one the map called Sarbak. And the jagged ridge standing a thousand feet above was unmistakable.

The warrior signaled the others to hold back, to spread out and lie down, to cover him. Then he walked toward the ridge, looking for signs of the main party, his concern growing with every step.

He had a second concern—that he'd be greeted by a burst of fire as he walked closer to somebody's foxhole. If a Karachistani patrol was here instead of the rest of the team, he'd be dead.

"Striker."

He turned to his right and saw Jan Huygen leaving his hiding place behind a cluster of rocks.

Both men glanced around and asked the same question. "Where are the others?"

"Our bunch is okay," Huygen replied. "Spread out. Under cover. Watching." He raised his hand and signaled. The others began to appear, some near at hand, others as much as a quarter of a mile away. "We didn't get here until about an hour ago," Huygen explained. "Patrols. Choppers. What about Ali, Sadir and the old man?"

Bolan swung his arm to call his group forward, telling how he'd left Ali and who Barnes was.

"I'm a little unhappy with the way our force has changed," Sokolov said to Bolan when they stood apart and talked a little later. "We know the people we brought with us. We know how much confidence we can place in them. But now we've got two Karachistanis, Suleiman and Raima, and we've got this soldier of fortune. Do you trust him?''

''Pass the word to our original people that Barnes has to be watched. No one's to turn his back on him.''

''Okay.'' The Russian nodded to the southwest and pointed. ''Raise your binoculars and look at about 190 degrees.''

Bolan did, peering at the distant, hazy horizon to the south. He was looking at the Surak Mountains, the last range before the sea. Between the Ashkab Mountains and the Suraks lay a broad green valley. The green was grass—sparse grass, according to their briefing, on which Karachistani herdsmen grazed many thousands of sheep and even a few cattle. To the west a big round lake sparkled in the sunlight—Lake Islan. And on the south shore of that lake, all but invisible in the haze and distance unless you knew what you were looking for and where to look for it, was Saravabad.

8

"We'll move at night," the Executioner told the team. "There's too much traffic down there for us to move during the day."

"Some of us can try it," Anahita Behzad replied. "Those of us who look like Karachistanis."

"In combat uniforms?" Barnes asked skeptically.

"I've got the accursed chador in my pack," she said.

"Anahita'll have to do some of the recon for us," Bolan said.

"As can I," Sadir volunteered. "I have a Karachistani peasant's clothes in my pack."

"If any of us are caught, it'll make no difference what we're wearing," Barnes told the group. "If any of Nassim's thugs nab us, we'll be branded spies and shot."

"Personally I don't plan to be taken alive," Bittrich stated.

"Neither do I," Sokolov added. "A cousin of mine

was captured in Afghanistan. I don't want to die the way he did."

"Okay," Bolan interrupted. "We've got a long march to reach Saravabad. They've shot another hostage. Who knows which one they'll kill next? So we don't have much time. Plan on moving. If anybody's concerned about being able to keep up, say so now."

Behzad translated this for Suleiman Zabara and his daughter. They shook their heads, and Suleiman murmured something quietly. "They say they can keep up," Behzad stated.

Bolan looked at Barnes.

"Don't worry about me, Striker."

THAT AFTERNOON they moved down the mountainside another few miles, then stopped and rested. After sunset, in weak yellow moonlight, they began their night march toward Nassim's new capital city.

They covered half the distance before the sun rose again. Huygen and Raima, scouting ahead, found an almost-dry wadi with not enough running water to attract shepherds and their flocks. It would serve as a campsite for the daylight hours, particularly in a curve where the rushing water that followed rainstorms had carved out a concave bank. Spread out in the shadow of that overhanging bank, they were invisible to all but those who approached within a few yards of them.

They spread out and sat in the shadow, first to eat rations, then to rest. Bolan took the first watch.

Elsewhere it would have been a pleasant, lazy day. The valley between the mountains was much like California or parts of Arizona. It was dry, with a hot sun, a wind churning up dust devils, yet with some green: scrub grass, scrub trees, whatever would grow under a punishing sun and with too little water.

The next night they covered another twenty or thirty miles of the valley until they were on the outskirts of the new city built to honor Hoshab Nassim. The old capital had been a city called Kartridgabad, a pleasant, palm-lined city on the Gulf of Oman. Afraid of assault from the sea, Hoshab Nassim had moved his capital to a city he built behind the Surak Mountains.

Although he proclaimed Saravabad a holy city in the pure tradition of Khariji Islam, it was, in fact, little more than a military camp, consisting chiefly of spare, Spartan prefab buildings with sides of pastel-enameled aluminum in shades of yellow and blue. Few of its streets were paved, and traffic raised a chronic cloud of dust that settled heavily on everything. The population was mostly Cobras and Wardens with their wives—and the usual assortment of prostitutes and other kinds of hustlers who came to serve the needs of the men stationed there.

The penalty for drinking alcohol in Saravabad was a hundred lashes—which some victims didn't survive—but alcohol sold briskly everywhere. That, Behzad told Bolan, characterized the city.

It was characterized also by the lack of a municipal water supply or a municipal sewage system, although most buildings were lighted by electricity and most of the city was connected by a telephone system. It was diligently policed by the Warden Believers, who enforced both civil and religious law.

There were just two permanent clusters of buildings in Saravabad. One was the mosque, which dominated the town. It stood in the center, a domed building with guardian minarets, sitting in the midst of a vast courtyard surrounded by the chief municipal buildings.

On the north side of the courtyard were the schools attended by young Karachistanis who were to learn the truths and glories of their faith, and also the power and dignity of Hoshab Nassim.

On the other side were the courts of law, where people went mostly to hear their disputes settled by bearded and learned men, the nation's experts in its particular version of Islamic law. Others, though, accused of crime, came in chains to hear their fates pronounced by the same stern men.

Men left the court wailing, some of them impoverished by decisions of the learned judges, some condemned in effect to slavery to pay their debts. Others howled in triumph. Occasionally a weeping woman walked stark naked out of the courtyard. If a man divorced his wife, he was entitled to reclaim everything he had ever given her, even the clothes on her back.

As punishment, men, occasionally women, were lashed to the point of death, some beyond that point. Hands were chopped off. Every week one or two received the ultimate penalty. They were held on their knees facing the mosque while an executioner chopped their heads off, which often took six or seven strokes to accomplish.

The second permanent cluster of buildings was Nassim's villa, which consisted of a luxurious palace and a surrounding group of outbuildings. It lay on the northwest edge of the city and on the shore of Lake Islan. For half a mile around no one could approach the estate, which was guarded by a special elite unit of the Karachistan Cobra Force. The villa's corridors and courtyards also swarmed with Warden Believers.

Before leaving the States the members of Bolan's team had studied satellite recon photos of the villa, and the Executioner carried a chart based on those pictures. The place had been built to be defended. It was surrounded by an eight-foot wall topped with coils of razor wire. There was only one gate, on the south side, which was flanked by guardhouses. The guardhouses—according to local intel—were equipped with machine guns and a variety of grenades. If anybody smashed the gate with a vehicle loaded with explosives, all he'd hit would be the guard headquarters building that stood immediately inside the gate.

The land inside the wall was well irrigated, and palm trees and tropical shrubs grew everywhere, although none so thick or high as to afford a man cover. Every square foot and corner of the property was illuminated by floodlights.

Behind the guard headquarters building was the palace, a long, low building consisting of east and west wings connected by narrow passageways. The center of the palace was a completely enclosed courtyard, also lush with trees and tropical shrubs, plus a big swimming pool made to look like a forest pool. It was irregular in shape and lined with stone, and water plants grew in and around it.

North of the palace was a one-story building that served as barracks for the Cobras and Wardens stationed inside the villa, and as a prison for Nassim's most important prisoners, such as the hostages he was now holding. The barracks and prison formed three sides of a courtyard—this one like a parade ground covered with dry sand and gravel.

The fourth side of this courtyard was a brick wall against which prisoners were stood to be shot by a firing squad.

From the beginning, during their briefings in the States, the team had understood the difficulty they would face in hitting this place hard enough and fast

enough to free the hostages before the Karachistani
dictator's forces could take them out.

It wasn't going to be easy.

THE NIGHT WAS COOL and the countryside wasn't difficult to cross. The team moved through flocks without disturbing them enough to raise an alarm. Once
they crossed a paved road.

"The main highway to Saravabad," Barnes commented.

As it turned out, Barnes was a good man to have
along. He hadn't spent as many years in Karachistan
as Behzad or Zabara and his daughter, but he had a
rough knowledge of the country. And, better than
that, it was the kind of knowledge a mercenary soldier picked up: where to purchase certain items, their
price. Also, he'd seen parts of Saravabad that Anahita and Raima, and most likely Suleiman, hadn't
seen: the sinks and brothels that weren't supposed to
exist, the barracks, the arsenals, the antiaircraft missile sites.

What was more, he was totally cynical. He didn't
hate the Karachistanis. His main aim was not to let
himself be outsmarted by them. Or defeated.

At dawn the team took refuge in two unroofed
barns of mud brick. When they were settled and the
first shift of sentries posted, Bolan went to Behzad and
told her he wanted to go into the city.

Half an hour later they left the barn and walked to the road—Behzad wearing a long black chador that covered her from head to toe, Bolan dressed in the tattered wool robe of a shepherd, with a turban wound for him by Sadir. His military boots would have given him away, so he had smeared his feet with dust and was wearing a pair of sandals Sadir had been carrying in the expectation that he, not Bolan, would to this probe. His face was tanned enough that his complexion wouldn't give him away, especially after a thorough rubbing of dust—although his blue eyes certainly would if he forgot to keep them cast down as he walked. Both he and Behzad carried Berettas under their robes.

From outside the city it was obvious that Saravabad was an artificial town with no real reason for existence other than Nassim's decree that it be built and that the government of Karachistan be conducted from there. In any real Karachistani town in the morning herders and farmers would be bringing their lambs to market, carrying a few vegetables, a little fruit, a few measures of corn. Merchants would be settling down in their places on the streets to sell the collection of odds and ends that typified Middle Eastern bazaars. The air should have been heavy with dust, the stink of manure, the perfume of strong coffee, the smells of street cooking.

Saravabad was different. The streets were lined with spare, square buildings, almost deserted except for detachments of Cobras and officious-looking men striding in a hurry from one building to another.

Only near the mosque was Saravabad anything like a normal Middle Eastern town. Near the mosque a few merchants squatted on the pavement, a few tiny shops offered coffee and tobacco, a few tethered lambs bawled in terror.

Entering the courtyard of the mosque, Bolan kept his eyes down, careful not to gaze into anyone's face. He appeared to be a mountain herder, a little fearful of the town, while Behzad was a subdued Khariji wife or daughter, peering out cautiously from behind her chador and following a respectful distance behind the man who governed her.

A cry of agony caught Bolan's attention. He jerked his head around and saw that a whipping had begun. A bearded man was bound to a post in the middle of the courtyard, naked except for a loincloth. The first stroke of the lash had cut a long bloody welt across his back. The whip descended again, and his blood flew. The man shrieked.

"Adulterer," Behzad murmured from behind Bolan's back. "They'll whip the woman next."

The warrior turned and walked out of the courtyard. A crowd was gathering, men pressing close. He didn't want to be caught in the middle of that. As well, the more men congregated to witness the lashings, the less there would be where he wanted to go.

He walked into a broad street that exited the court-yard to the east, then turned left into another broad street that led north. At the end of that street, two hundred yards away, he could see the high, wire-topped wall and the guarded gate of Nassim's palace.

He headed toward it, Behzad at his side. The compound resembled a prison more than a palace. The coils of razor wire glinted in the morning sun. Guards stood behind glass in the towers to either side of the gate. Lights were mounted on tripods on the walls.

Although the gate stood wide open, an armored vehicle equipped with machine guns and a cannon was parked in front of it.

Adopting the type of humble shuffle he'd observed among the simple desert people who had ventured into this garrison town, the warrior moved north toward the lakeshore.

"You can't look stupid enough to be allowed to walk around this place," she muttered.

"Maybe." He told her what to say if they were stopped.

They proceeded to the end of the street and stood opposite the gate, three hundred feet distant across a clearing. Bolan shuffled off to his right and walked to the southeast corner of the palace compound. Then he headed north, keeping to the edge of the cleared land but close enough to the wall to observe the gun emplacements on the roof of the building he identified as the palace.

It was plain that Hoshab Nassim didn't trust anybody—not even his own people, who were supposed to worship him. Obviously he didn't place much trust in God, either. His trust was in armored cars, machine guns, radar and missiles.

At the north end of the palace compound, a hundred yards from the shore of Lake Islan, Bolan turned left and walked along the north wall of the palace compound a little closer than before, since here he was closer to what the recon photos indicated was the building where the hostages were held.

Three Warden Believers stepped through a small narrow door in the wall and swaggered across the barren land toward what looked like an old country man and his woman.

Bolan began to bow and smile, his right hand on his Beretta. Behzad talked. She spoke with the elaborate deference usually afforded ayatollahs. Her head bobbed as she spoke quietly and respectfully. The Wardens—in their khakis and red berets—stood with their hips cocked and listened with unmistakable scorn.

After a long moment of conversation, the apparent leader of the three Wardens swung his arm and stalked away toward the door in the wall.

"What did you say to them?" Bolan asked.

"What you told me to say," she said. "I told them that my elderly father begged the privilege of being allowed to walk one time all the way around the sacred home of the exalted Hoshab Nassim, as the Faithful walk around the holy places in Mecca. And you know what?"

"What?"

"Those idiots believed it."

Bolan laughed, but he bowed his head low and began his slow shuffle again. "Let's be glad they're not too smart. This is going to be a tough nut to crack."

HOSHAB NASSIM SAT on a sagging aluminum-and-plastic chaise lounge beside the pool in the courtyard of his palace, drinking from a black bottle of Napoleon brandy in defiance of the Prophet's law, an offense that would earn one of his subjects a hundred lashes and maybe a lingering, agonizing death. Also within reach was a generous supply of the white dust that brought instant, if not permanent, ecstasy. He was naked.

This was what victory brought a man. The fruits of victory, they called it. All a man wanted, of whatever he wanted. And it was so valuable that a man was ready to do whatever he had to do to keep it.

His women sat around the pool, three of them his wives. He wasn't absolutely sure which ones. The new one thought he didn't know that she was an American.

That beautiful body, so smooth, so perfectly configured ... He'd decided he would treat her as a man would treat a fine racehorse: feed and exercise her most carefully, cultivate all that was best in her, not demand too much of her and enjoy all she had to offer, the way he enjoyed the Napoleon brandy.

It was difficult to talk with her. She had learned Arabic to accommodate her late husband, but she didn't speak it well, while he, Hoshab Nassim, spoke it hardly at all. No matter. He would speak to her in another language for now.

The hostage venture hadn't worked out well. He had two choices now: to dispose of the rest of them—not Sauda, of course—and let the world write them off as the cost of discovering that Hoshab Nassim meant what he said, or negotiating some sort of release for them.

He couldn't let them go without a valuable— What did the infidels say? A valuable quid pro quo. If he did, that would admit defeat. And Hoshab Nassim was *never* defeated.

SAUDA STARED at Nassim, hatred burning in her eyes. Yes, she'd had to surrender to him, but it had been nothing. He hadn't touched her soul.

He had trouble. The Masoudi, north of the Ash-kab Mountains, had once again risen in rebellion. They'd wiped out a Guardian station to the man and had somehow gotten their hands on missiles and had brought down a helicopter. He had sent major forces into the desert north of the mountains, and so far the reports didn't suggest victory.

To the contrary. Karachistan Defense Force troops had killed a score of Masoudi tribesmen and had found no evidence of their new weapons, not even evidence of the new leadership that had to be in place, directing their newly effective attacks.

Shortly, if the rumor she had heard from a tiny, whip-scarred woman was right, the brave dictator would be leaving the palace soon. Afraid of an attack on the compound, he was going to move out into the mountains somewhere to sleep in a hut or a tent. Also, if the woman was right, she, Sauda, was to go with him. She was his newest, and she had his interest.

She hadn't dared ask him why he'd killed Ibrahim. In time she would find out. Somehow, some way, she would find out. And then…well, then she might find a way to relieve mankind of the curse of Hoshab Nassim.

9

Suleiman Zabara and his daughter Raima, the fourth wife of Hoshab Nassim, insisted they would accompany the team in its assault on the palace. At first Bolan refused. He wasn't persuaded by their insistence, translated by Behzad, that they would be useful. But he was finally convinced by the argument, made by Raima, that if they were separated from what she now called her comrades, they would surely be captured and tortured to death.

So once the last glow of sunset had faded and the sky was black, with the moon casting a faint light over the landscape, the team left the refuge of the ruined granary buildings and spread out for its approach to the city and the palace.

They were ten—against what? Legions of Warden Believers and Cobras?

Their best intel said that the hostages were kept in the building just inside the north wall. But that could be wrong. The hostages might have been removed from the palace compound.

And there was no way to find out.

IN ONE WAY Saravabad was like any garrison town. Cobras were in the bars and cribs, drinking the alcohol that both civil and religious law strictly forbade, frolicking with the prostitutes that were even more strictly forbidden. In another way it was different. The laws were so rigid, the punishments so savage, that men moved through the streets with extreme caution. Warden Believers drank, too, and used the services of the prostitutes, but no one could be sure which one of them might be such a fanatic as to sound the alarm and call down the penalties of the law.

"The men of the Karachistan Cobra Force despise the Warden Believers," Barnes told Bolan. "Every week or so a Warden is found dead somewhere in town."

Moving into the outskirts of the little city, the team spotted Wardens and Cobras moving furtively on the streets. It was almost impossible to tell which ones were sneaking to one kind of rendezvous or another and which ones were patrols—except that some of them were conspicuously drunk. The combat team didn't want to encounter either kind, but they wouldn't be able to avoid them all.

Bolan took point while the team followed in two lines, one on either side of the streets they traveled toward the palace compound. Keeping in the shadows on dimly lighted streets, they were able to pass six pairs of Wardens and half a dozen little knots of Cobras without being noticed.

But without warning a bearded man in khaki and wearing the red beret of the Warden Believers stepped out of a doorway and raised his hand. He grunted something.

"He says halt," muttered Barnes, who was following immediately behind Bolan.

The Executioner stopped and confronted the Warden. The man squinted at him and for a long moment didn't seem to understand what he was looking at, didn't seem to notice the SIG 550 in the warrior's hand, nor the combat clothes. Maybe the darkness confused him, or he thought Bolan was a member of the Cobra Force.

He spoke again, this time louder, and another Warden moved from the shadows, then a third.

"No gunfire," Bolan said firmly and quietly to Barnes.

"You got it, Striker, but I don't see how the hell—"

The Warden Believer with the beard barked a harsh order.

"He wants us to shut up," Barnes translated. The Warden went on snarling, and Barnes said, "He just noticed me. I don't look like I belong here. I make him nervous."

At that instant the Warden Believer reached for the pistol holstered on his hip. Bolan's bayonet swept up, stabbed into the man's abdomen and lifted him off his feet. The warrior pushed the corpse onto a second Warden, who went down under the weight.

Barnes was quick. He didn't fire his Uzi, merely slammed it into the face of the third Karachistani—nine pounds of hard steel crashing into the man's nose. He went down, and Barnes stepped back one pace and kicked the second Warden, who was shrugging off the weight of his comrade. The merc's boot caught that Warden alongside the ear, and he dropped back onto the pavement.

Huygen moved in, lunged and drove his bayonet into the Warden with the broken nose.

It was over. Quietly.

"Move," Bolan ordered. "We don't need to clean up."

Barnes took a moment to pull a Browning automatic from the holster of one of the bodies. "Noticed this," he said. "I'm not going to leave anything this good lying on the street."

THE PALACE COMPOUND was even more formidable at night than during the day. The lights glared on the walls. The hundred-yard strip of land around the compound was brightly illuminated.

"I assume," Bittrich said, "that land isn't seeded with mines. Given mines and ferocious dogs, it would look like the old sector border between the two Germanys."

"No mines," Barnes replied. "I've seen sheep herded across that land."

They were situated to the east, not far from the shore of Lake Islan. Boats with yellow lanterns hung on their cabins bobbed on the gently swelling waters of the lake, fishermen hoping for a nighttime catch. They had one chance, and they knew it. The attack on the palace compound had to be quick and devastating. They had to hit hard, so hard that the defenders would at first panic and would take time to recover and organize. When the Warden Believers and the men of Cobra Force regrouped, their far superior numbers could easily repel the combat team. Success—and survival—depended on a fast, overpowering strike and a quick withdrawal.

That was what they had planned. All that remained was its execution.

The sharpshooter had the first job. The explosives man the second. Neither was easy.

McCulloch stretched out on the ground just beyond reach of the glaring floodlights. He settled into position, extended the bipod legs on his SIG 550 rifle and snapped the telescopic sight into place.

"One hundred yards," Bolan told him. "That's what I figure from this morning's recon."

McCulloch nodded. Having the distance more exact than a guestimate was an advantage. Using one of the click knobs, he adjusted the sight. The wall was about eight feet high, and the tripods that held the floodlights were about four feet—roughly four yards from ground to lights, so he set the elevation accordingly. The wind was calm and came from behind him. He left the windage at zero. Then he set the rifle to fire single shots. "Ready."

Bolan turned to Ardeshir Sadir, who had been squatting on the ground making a final check of the explosive charge he had assembled in the ruined granary that afternoon. He looked up at the Executioner and nodded.

"Okay, Doug," Bolan said. "It's yours."

There were two lights that had to be taken out for sure: one on the northeast corner and one on the eastern wall. McCulloch took long and careful aim on the corner light. Its glare came hard through the scope, and he winced as it struck his eye. He couldn't focus on it long; his eye couldn't take it. He applied gentle yet firm pressure on the trigger. He had experience with the SIG 550 and knew what the weapon could do. It was smooth. He could feel in the trigger just when it was about to fire. And it did, just when he expected it.

The corner floodlight exploded and went dark, followed by a shout. Somebody in a guard station had been hit by glass or was yelling an alarm.

Sadir rose to a crouch, as did Bolan and Bittrich. McCulloch squeezed off his second shot, and the east wall floodlight exploded. Now they knew they were under attack.

Sadir sprinted for the east wall, carrying his explosive charge. Bolan was with him, and Bittrich was only a pace or two behind. They were his cover.

A hundred yards could be covered easily in fifteen seconds if a man was in top shape. For men running for their lives it would seem an eternity.

The defenders were gathering. The alarm had been given and the leaders of the troops were yelling commands.

The Marine fired a third shot, going for a spotlight on the roof of the palace. And he got it.

Return fire poured from the compound, wild shots, automatic weapons fire, directed at the sudden darkness. Something had to be coming from the darkness out there, and the defenders filled it with flying steel.

The Karachistanis were at a disadvantage. They had been inside the glare from their spotlights, and their eyes needed time to adjust. The assault team had been in the darkness. The moonlight was enough illumination for them, for the moment.

Sadir screamed, then pitched forward onto his face, silent. Bolan dropped beside him, ten yards from the wall. Bittrich never stopped. He ran past them, snatching up the explosive charge in its canvas satchel, and dashed for the base of the wall.

Sadir was dead. Bolan could see that plainly enough. He'd been hit in the face. There was nothing he could do.

Bittrich had left the satchel in position and raced to Bolan's side. "Let's go!"

The two men were almost halfway back to the rest of the team when the blast threw them onto their faces. Sadir had done his job well. The blast had shot bricks and mortar hundreds of feet into the air, and the debris pounded to the earth in a lethal shower. A significant chunk of the wall had vanished.

Bolan and Bittrich lay on the ground, heaving, the breath knocked out of them. The team had its orders and, everyone knowing exactly what to do, raced past them, firing bursts into the gap in the wall.

Raima stopped and knelt over Bolan. She spoke urgently but in Urdu, and all he could do was smile at her as he struggled to his feet. She grabbed him and tried to help him. He wanted to caution her and her father not to run wildly into the fire zone, but as soon as she saw he was up and moving, she sprinted for the wall.

The others were through the breach. With a few quick bursts they cleared the inside of the compound—as far as it could be cleared.

The blast that took down the wall had also taken down part of the wall of the barracks-prison. The team had to hold its fire, as no one knew if the near rooms housed Wardens or the hostages. They tossed grenades onto the roof. Furiously driven shot cleared anyone who was up there.

When Bolan jumped through the gap and into the compound, Mikhail Sokolov was already carrying out the second element of the attack plan. On his knees he aimed an Armbrust at the palace, then fired the missile. Armor-piercing, it penetrated the palace wall before a kilogram of high explosive detonated, blasting away a corner off the palace, lifting the roof and filling the whole east wing of the palace with smoke and terror.

Then Behzad fired a second round, this one into the center of the palace. It punched through the north wall and detonated when it hit the south, across the inside corridor, above the courtyard and swimming pool. An eruption of bricks and mortar flew into the courtyard. The roof sagged.

The idea was to make the defenders believe the target was Nassim, not his hostages. It worked. Soldiers raced from the west end of the barracks-prison, sprinting for the palace itself and to the defense of their leader.

Bolan led the team into the barracks-prison. The building was dark and filled with smoke. They realized at once that they weren't in the prison part. They had to work their way west through the building.

Defenders? Probably. A good way to get them out was to continue the deception that the target of the attack was the palace. The recon pictures had suggested that the distance between barracks-prison and palace, on the south side, wasn't great. In fact, it wasn't. Huygen knelt in a window of the barracks and blasted out a palace window with his SIG 550. Then he pitched a grenade through the opening and into the ground floor of the palace.

Bittrich knew the plan and did the same. Once again the palace shuddered with blast and fire.

Bolan and Behzad forced their way west. And in the prison wing of the barracks building they found the hostages.

The first one they found was Colonel Ilinsky. Crouched on the floor in a dark cell half filled with smoke and dust, he was still chained to a heavy hunk of steel, which he'd dragged to a corner of the room.

Bolan spoke to him. When the man replied in a swift Russian dialect, the Executioner couldn't understand.

"Mikhail!" he called. "Barnes! Bittrich!"

Sokolov ran into the room. He turned a flashlight on the Russian and began to talk to him. Barnes entered carrying Sadir's kit, which had the stuff they would use to cut the chains off the prisoners.

Bittrich joined them. Bolan pointed to the chain on the Russian's leg, and the German nodded and began to poke around inside Sadir's canvas bag.

They had anticipated finding the hostages in chains and the necessity of cutting them off quick. Sadir had brought a pyrolitic magnesium compound that was something like the thermite that had once been used in welding. It consisted of powdered magnesium, powdered aluminum and an acid bound together in a type of putty. Bittrich had used the stuff before, so he knelt and performed the operation.

He ripped the paper covering off the putty, then kneaded the material into a glob around one of the links in the chain. Also in the package was a fuse, a thin strip of magnesium with a chemical igniter like an oversize match head. Bittrich pushed the strip deep into the glob and touched the flame of a lighter to the igniter, which flared. Its heat ignited the magnesium strip, which burned with bright white light. In a few seconds the white flame reached the putty glob, which burst into a larger white flame, sending up a cloud of poisonous smoke. Ready for this, Bolan and Sokolov fanned the air with their jackets to disperse the deadly fumes. The putty burned fiercely for a quarter of a minute.

The intense heat melted the steel of the link inside the glob, and the chain separated. A stream of slugs ripped down the corridor outside the cells, ricocheting off the walls and floor. One of the team members answered with a burst of fire, then with a grenade thrown from a window into the area between the building and the main wall.

Sokolov turned to Bolan. "This man is Colonel Ilinsky. He says your CIA man, Craig, is in the third cell along the passageway."

Bolan nodded, grabbing another pack of the magnesium compounds from Sadir's bag. McCulloch was at a door in the west end of the building, providing cover against any more bursts of gunfire from the defenders. As Bolan trotted toward the third cell, McCulloch fired at a figure running toward the building and dropped him. He fired also on the floodlights on the west wall, and at this close range he took them out one after another.

Craig was a mess. His nose was a smashed, distorted mass of scabby, swollen flesh. His cheekbone was broken. Obviously he'd been beaten and not been given medical attention. He sat slumped on a wooden bench, what apparently served as his cot, his wrists and ankles heavily chained.

"Craig?"

Robert Craig raised his eyes and squinted at the Executioner. "My God! Bolan!"

They had run into each other years ago during Bolan's Mafia war.

"Just call me Striker."

"Understood."

"We haven't got much time. I'm going to burn your leg chain in two. The chain on your wrists will have to come later. Hold your legs as far apart as you can."

Craig did as he was told, and Bolan kneaded the putty around a link.

"I've been told you're not the only American here," Bolan stated.

"There was another American," Craig replied, staring as Bolan lit the fuse and the lump of putty burst into white-hot flame. "They shot the Sudanese. Then they took his wife away someplace. I don't know where."

"That leaves six of you here, then."

Craig nodded as he pulled his legs wide apart. "There's a man here named Nathan Block. He's a Mossad agent. So was Sadik, the Sudanese they shot. We've got a lot to talk about, my friend."

"Yeah, but it'll have to be later."

The warrior stepped out into the corridor. Bittrich had now freed the second Russian, Kamensky from his shackles, and he was with Ilinsky, stumbling around uncertainly. Suleiman Zabara had observed the procedure and had burned the chains off the Iranian and the Iraqi.

Behzad was talking with the Iranian, but she didn't speak Arabic, which was the only language the Iraqi spoke. He stood fearful and confused, pressing his back to a wall. Bolan could speak some Arabic, and let the man know that he was being rescued.

Or was he? Firing from the direction of the palace itself had increased. Heavy stuff. Machine guns on the roof likely. The brick walls of the barrack and prison shuddered, and pieces began to fall away.

It was time to get out, but Bittrich was having difficulty with the shackles on the legs of the Mossad agent, Block. What had to be cut wasn't a link in a chain but a heavy steel bar. Bittrich had put two packages of the putty around the bar, but he was afraid the heat would pass through the bar to the man's ankles and burn him severely.

Ilinsky came running along the corridor carrying a bucket of water from the latrine. The other Russian had torn off his shirt and was wrapping it around Block's left ankle. The Iranian saw what was happening and tore off his to wrap around Block's right ankle. Ilinsky soaked the shirts with water from the bucket.

A burst of heavy slugs tore through the ceiling and showered dust on all of them.

"Another Armbrust?" Behzad asked Bolan.

''Not unless we have to. We'll need them against the helicopters.''

Bittrich lit the fuse, and the putty flared. Block groaned, and Ilinsky splashed water on his ankles. Bolan and Behzad whipped their shirts back and forth to fan away the fumes.

The bar separated. When Ilinsky threw water on the severed ends, steam rose.

Block grimaced in pain. The Russian raced away to get another bucket of water but met Raima coming with a bucket. He grabbed it from her and threw it onto the Israeli's legs.

They couldn't leave the palace compound through the hole they'd blasted through the wall. The defenders had already blocked it. The armored car from the front of the compound had been moved just outside the gap in the wall, machine guns and cannon aimed and ready.

McCulloch threw himself onto the ground outside the west door he'd been guarding and sprayed the area between the palace and the wall with sustained bursts from his SIG 550, as did Sokolov, who fired at the palace roof.

Bittrich came forward with another charge of plastique hanging around his neck by its quick-burning fuse. He lit the fuse, sprinted across the open space to the wall, shoved the charge into place and ran for cover. The explosive charge went off with a roar that collapsed the west wall of the prison wing and its roof.

Running outside, Bolan saw the results of Bittrich's handiwork—a gaping hole in the main wall, their way out. He trotted to the south corner of the prison wing, where he pitched two grenades toward the palace. They sailed through the shattered remains of a window and went off. The west wing of the palace filled with smoke and dust.

Sokolov and Behzad led the hostages across the open space between the prison wing and the newly created hole in the wall. The six hostages moved awkwardly, their loose chains whipping the ground. Barnes and the Executioner stayed inside the wall until everyone else was out, discouraging the Wardens and Cobras with quick, accurate bursts of fire.

Suddenly it was over. They were out of the palace compound. But Saravabad was alive with forces moving in for the kill.

THE SURAK MOUNTAINS to the south of Saravabad weren't nearly as formidable a chain as the Ashkabs. The mountain ridge was sharp, though, and climbing could be more difficult.

To Hoshab Nassim the Surak Mountains were home. His father had herded goats there, as had his father before him. It was where the young Nassim had grown up and the home he'd left when he joined the army. It was where he had married his first wife, where she had borne his first son. And it was his refuge.

And tonight he needed a refuge.

He stood just outside his long black Mercedes limousine, the wind fluttering the cotton robe he wore over his khaki uniform as general of the Karachistani army. He held a pair of binoculars to his eyes, and he stared back at Saravabad, only ten kilometers north and a thousand meters below.

His palace was burning. He could see the flashes of explosions and salvos of sparks flying up into the sky. An army had attacked. He'd been wise to leave the city this evening. He'd known instinctively that tonight the satanic enemy would attack.

Maybe five thousand men. An airborne division, without doubt, that had dropped on the valley east of Lake Islan and moved in with overwhelming force.

The radar operators insisted no air armada had violated Karachistani airspace. They failed to take into account the devilish electronic countermeasures the Evil One had placed at the disposal of his forces.

This was the invasion. It was what he had prepared for all these years. They had tried to deceive him with a feint in the north, to make him believe the operation was nothing more than another Masoudi uprising. His deputy commanders had sent forces north without consulting him. Now they were frantically recalling them. Detachments of the Cobra Force were racing south through the pass. The army, lethargic as always, would be slower to respond.

But from here, in his home mountains, where he could observe the fighting below, he, Hoshab Nassim, would direct his forces to their inevitable victory.

A servant hurried forward and handed a bottle of brandy to one of his women. It was the American one who accepted it, Sauda, the one whose husband had come to Karachistan to overthrow the state. The best of them. The best of his women. For the moment. If he didn't soon recapture and tame the rebellious Raima, daughter of the fiendish Suleiman Zabara, he would divorce her and, under the law of the Prophet, he could take to wife another woman, maybe the dark one, Sauda.

SHE DIDN'T THINK of herself as Sauda anymore. She was Melanie Helms from Newark, New Jersey. And the man who had ordered her husband's death had no idea how well an American woman could hate. The abused Karachistani women didn't dare hate their lords and masters: men, the chosen of God. So he didn't suspect how much she hated him, how she longed for a chance to hurt him. To hurt him…to kill him.

She shuffled forward to hand him his brandy—shuffled because he had ordered leg irons locked onto her ankles again, obviously suspecting she might try to run away from him the way his fourth wife had done.

She lowered her eyes and handed him the brandy. Lowering her eyes was no mark of respect. It was to hide her hatred and contempt.

Down below his palace was blowing up before his eyes. She wondered if any of the other hostages had survived the attack.

10

The job wasn't half done. They had accomplished the easiest part.

They had come into Karachistan with two alternative plans. One plan called for them to move around the western shore of Lake Islan and order in Navy choppers to pick them up. At least one American aircraft carrier was stationed off the Strait of Hormuz—there, as usual, guarding the strait, and alerted to monitor the frequency on which an international antiterrorist team might call for evacuation. Fast helicopters launched from the right place could reach the western shore of the lake in thirty minutes.

The second plan was for them to cross the Surak Mountains and make their way down to the coast. The problem was, they had lost their radios in the drop. Every one of them. Although they had been dispersed in three packs, every radio had been smashed.

Bolan considered his options as he strode ahead of the others, moving out of Saravabad to the west through narrow streets that so far stayed quiet. This was the original village, what had existed before Nassim had decided to make Saravabad his capital.

The pickup by helicopters west of the lake would be a touchy operation. It involved violation of Karachistani airspace and a quick, precise operation. Without communication.

The warrior decided they had to move south, up the steep slopes and over the jagged peak of the Surak Mountains. But first they had to get away from Saravabad.

The palace was burning. The Armbrusts and grenades had set fires, and the Cobras and Wardens were making no apparent effort to put them out.

The stutter of automatic small-arms fire was constant, punctuated by occasional explosions. Unmuffled engines roared—not the engines of trucks bringing up detachments, but those of armored vehicles, perhaps small tanks.

Also the choppers. Hoshab Nassim seemed to have believed the secret of war was helicopters. He had a lot of them, and they had swarmed in from all around, twenty of them over Saravabad.

But for the moment nothing was coordinated. The choppers swung over the little city, some of them sweeping the streets with airborne floodlights, none of them within a mile of where Bolan was leading his people away to the west. As for the heavy fire, the soldiers had to be shooting at one another, if they were shooting at anything.

But none of this was to be scorned. Sooner or later they would get their act together.

Behzad hurried to Bolan's side. "That's Highway 6," she said, pointing to a narrow road with broken pavement. "It goes south into the mountains. There's not much but rough country between here and the Iranian border. The highway at least keeps to country you can travel through."

The highway also ran through the town, not through the open rough country to the west, where they could have moved less conspicuously. But there was no choice. The Executioner swung his arm around and led his people south on Highway 6.

So far the shooting was focused over the center of Saravabad and the palace. Bolan would have liked to urge his people into a trot, to put distance between them and the palace, but he knew the hostages couldn't run. He strode as far out ahead of them as he dared, then looked back to see them strung out for a hundred yards behind him, some of his team lagging back to help the struggling men.

A helicopter roared overhead, so low they could see the open doors and the machine guns aimed toward the ground. It passed barely fifty feet above the roofs of the shabby little buildings that lined the streets.

Then it had to happen. A dozen soldiers, trotting through an intersection ahead of them, peered around, staring into streets lighted by nothing but moonlight. Bolan swung his arms to signal his team to split to the two sides of the street.

They did, and the squad seemed at first to miss them. Then a man yelled.

The soldiers dropped to the pavement and opened fire. Bolan swept a burst over the pavement just in front of them, sending whining, ricocheting slugs among them—a sound that terrified the bravest men. His people opened fire from behind him. Bittrich heaved a grenade that exploded in the midst of the squad, and it was over.

The hostages plundered the squad, pulling the weapons from their hands, arming themselves to be part of their own rescue. Bolan watched the Iraqi pull the combat boots off one Warden and trot off with them slung around his neck. They would be a useful replacement for the man's worn, loose sandals.

"Move!" Bolan shouted.

He knew the sound of gunfire would draw more squads. In fact, he heard yelling in a street not more than a block away. He hung back now and let Sokolov lead the group south on the highway, while he and Huygen stayed behind to discourage pursuers.

And they got their chance. Six more Wardens jogged recklessly into the intersection—and into deadly bursts from Bolan and Huygen.

Now the two men took the time to check the dead. They weren't carrying unlimited ammo, and this night's battle had depleted their stock. The 5.56 mm ammo cycled by the SIG 550s was a standard caliber, and they found that some of the Wardens had been carrying weapons chambered for the same rounds. They trotted away three minutes later with another two hundred bullets. What was more, Bolan shoved a Walther PPK into a pocket, a useful little pistol that might come in handy sometime.

They caught up with the rest of the group. The sounds of battle in the streets had brought people to the windows, and faces stared at the odd assortment of men and women hurrying past. They made Bolan tense. If they started shooting from windows...

But no one did. The people had no idea what was going on or who the men and women in the street might be.

An armored car lumbered around a corner to the north and sped through the street toward the team. It was a big vehicle, riding tall on huge solid rubber tires. Its headlights glared.

Bolan took an Armbrust from Raima, who was carrying two of them, and crouched to fire. But the driver of the armored car was in too big a hurry to notice a few men and women in the street. He was looking for a regiment, and he rushed past without slowing down.

The Executioner led his group through two more blocks without encountering anything dangerous. Behzad moved up to walk beside him. "They'll set up roadblocks on every road out of town, in all directions," she told him. "When I lived here, every time there was excitement they blocked every road."

Bolan nodded. "Thanks for the warning."

Craig wanted to talk and hurried to catch up with Bolan. When Behzad dropped back, he asked, "Who's the American in civilian clothes?"

"Ever hear of a guy named Gib Barnes?"

"Yeah. A mercenary."

"He's with me. A couple of Wardens had him. He says you're not the only American hostage."

"There was a Sudanese couple. They shot the husband and took the wife away somewhere. The wife's an American. I'm sure they don't know that. It's not why they shot her husband."

"Barnes was hired to try to arrange an escape for the Sudanese," Bolan said.

Craig shook his head. "Barnes was hired to arrange the death of the Sudanese. And probably did."

"Because he worked for the Mossad?"

"Right. He knew too much to let them break him—and they were breaking him by torturing his wife. The

Karachistanis don't know Block's with the Mossad, and I doubt they knew the Sudanese was. They know I'm CIA, or strongly suspect it, but I don't think they know the Mossad connection.''

''Barnes says one of the hostages has got to be a traitor,'' Bolan said.

''He would.''

''How would Barnes have known the Sudanese was about to break? Block would have known.''

''I thought of that,'' Craig replied. ''But what could Block have told the Karachistanis to make them want to shoot the Sudanese?''

Bolan shrugged. ''What could Barnes have told them?''

''We better keep an eye on both of them.''

HIGHWAY 6 RAN OUT OF TOWN. Less than an hour after they left the palace compound the team and the hostages were in almost open country. Buildings and sheds stood on both sides of the road, some a few yards off the road at the ends of rutted drives. The highway itself was only a narrow strip of cracked macadam, rutted in places where the wheels of heavy trucks had simply broken through. In places it was covered in sand, left there by the desert wind.

There were no lights. The buildings and sheds were dark. The only illumination was provided by the moon, which was now coldly bright and shed enough light to see by.

Bolan set McCulloch and Huygen fifty yards to his left and right, and the three of them moved out a hundred yards ahead of the other twelve.

"Nobody fires a weapon without orders," he said before he moved out. "Shots fired out here could bring the whole Karachistani army down on us."

Two miles out of town he spotted the roadblock. An armored car had been parked in the middle of the road. Two trucks sat behind it. The warrior could see twenty or more men, a detachment of the Cobra Force. And if he could see twenty, there had to be twice that many more, spread out on both sides in a skirmish line.

McCulloch and Huygen had read the situation, too. The big Marine trotted back to stop the others. Bolan and Huygen squatted beside the road.

"Can't fight our way through," the Dutchman said. "Too many of them. Country's too open."

"Besides which, they'll call in reinforcements."

"We have to go around," Huygen decided.

"Maybe they've thrown a line all around the town," Bolan replied. "I think we've got to find a hole. Or make one."

"Let me go and see what—"

"I'll do it," Bolan interrupted. "I want the crowd off the road, lying low back out of sight from the pavement. You and Doug back me up. I'll do a probe. Keep back but don't lose me.''

BOLAN WORKED his way forward cautiously. The Karachistanis smoked cigarettes. That was an advantage. The flare of a match, the point of orange fire, made a man a target. As he crept forward, Bolan spotted several cigarettes to his right and left.

Dead ahead there was nothing. But it was too big a gap. There had to be a man in the gap between the smokers to both sides.

A helicopter flew over. It wouldn't bother his team, but it would distract the attention of the Cobras. There had to be a man just ahead. That was how they were spaced. The warrior peered into the pale, cold moonlight and listened.

A sound . . . Bolan held himself alert and listened.

Sometime, sooner or later, a man had to relieve his bladder, even if he was on guard duty. And when he did, that splashing sound was unmistakable.

And pinpointed him for an experienced soldier making a probe.

Now that he knew where to look, the moonlight was enough to locate the man for Bolan. A shadow. Where there were no trees, a standing man was obvious when you knew where to look.

Bolan placed the SIG 550 assault rifle on the ground. He knew he didn't dare fire it, and carrying the weapon could only impede him. He drew his silenced Beretta and stuck it in his belt, then unsheathed his deadly combat knife, the Bali-Song.

Carefully judging the terrain between him and the Cobra, the warrior crept forward. He could see the man now. The soldier held a short automatic weapon cradled in his left arm, with his right hand on the pistol grip. He was alert. As the guy turned, Bolan spotted the coiled black cobra sewed around one sleeve.

Meant to scare people. And probably did.

Bolan inched his way closer, pausing after his every move to judge whether or not the Cobra had heard him. He was careful of every stone he touched, every stunted weed.

He unfolded the Bali-Song, locking the handles to make an L—with the blade at a ninety-degree angle to the handles.

Now he rose and set himself to lunge. The Cobra looked to his right and left. For an instant his eyes seemed to settle on the shadowy figure of the Executioner, but he didn't tense or raise the muzzle of his weapon. He turned away.

In an instant Bolan was on top of the man, driving the point of the knife into his throat. The L set of the blade and handles made it easy to pull the buried blade back and across, cutting through arteries. His left hand covered the soldier's mouth, making sure he died quietly. When the death struggles ceased, he lowered the corpse to the ground.

Now, if he'd guessed right, he had a gap in the line. Bolan squatted beside the dead man, scanning the immediate vicinity, listening. Nothing. Silence. Except to his rear, to the north. He tensed, then relaxed, knowing that it was Huygen. Before the Dutchman reached him Bolan signaled to go back and get the rest of the team.

The warrior stepped back a few paces and picked up his rifle. McCulloch crept forward, and for a moment Bolan spoke to him in a whisper. The Marine nodded and moved out, starting a soft probe of the terrain beyond the line.

A minute later Barnes advanced, leading Raima and Craig. He saluted the Executioner with his Uzi and without a word led his charges south. Next came Bittrich with the two Russians, Ilinsky and Kamensky.

Seven were now past the line the Cobras had set up to the east and west of their roadblock. Good enough.

But a voice carried to him from the east, the direction of the road, a man saying something in the language of the country. An officer, a guy checking his line and the men he'd positioned out here.

Bolan stared into the dark. He couldn't see the guy, or the remainder of his advancing team. He guessed he could be confident he wouldn't, not until this problem was taken care of. Huygen was hanging back as traffic cop, and the Dutchman was a pro.

Bolan straightened the Bali-Song into the regular knife configuration. He could count on something. When the officer found the body of his soldier, his attention would be focused for a moment—which would give the warrior his chance.

The guy strode along, muttering something under his breath, hurrying impatiently, his boots crunching on the hard ground. He called out, irritation in his voice.

And the Executioner struck. The blade pierced between the Cobra's ribs once, was pulled out, then went in again. Bolan's hard left arm crushed the guy's throat, cutting off his breath and voice. The officer went limp and slipped to the ground.

Behzad, Suleiman and Block hurried past, followed by Sokolov with the Iranian and the Iraqi.

Huygen joined Bolan. "We're through."

He and the Executioner headed south. Sokolov and McCulloch had the group hugging the ground, spread out for more safety.

Behzad spoke to Bolan. "See the lights on the mountain crest ahead of us? They belong to some of Nassim's radar stations and missile emplacements. Well guarded, you can be sure. We can't get past in the daylight. What's more, we've got a tough climb. That's steep."

Bolan stood staring at the mountains, no more than ten miles away. He nodded. "We need to find cover for daylight."

A pair of helicopters flew south from Saravabad, directly above Highway 6, flooding the road and the land to each side with light. They rushed past, not searching for anything, as though they were on an urgent mission.

11

By first light of dawn the team and the hostages were less than a third of the way up the north slope of the Surak Mountains, about five miles from the outskirts of the city. They had fought their way up steep rocks, the stronger among them helping the weaker. When the moon set and there was no light, they'd had to stop; it was impossible to climb the mountain terrain in the dark. As well, some of the hostages were totally exhausted and dropped gratefully to the ground when Mack Bolan called a halt.

The mountainside offered plenty of cover, but provided neither water nor food. Bolan put Mikhail Sokolov in charge of rationing what they had.

As the sun rose, casting long shadows over the valley below, Bolan sat with Huygen and Behzad, and they studied the vista spread out below and behind them.

A tall column of gray smoke rose from the palace and drifted away on the wind. Clouds of dust marked columns of vehicles moving across the valley.

"They're looking for us," Behzad stated.

"Not yet," Bolan replied. "What they're looking for is a big force. That's an army down there, maneuvering to meet a battalion."

She nodded. "Some of them know we were only a few, but their egos won't let them believe a small team freed Nassim's hostages and set fire to his palace. I bet they're claiming Karachistan was invaded last night."

"They'll eventually figure it out," Bolan said. "They'll be coming up here."

"How are we going to get out of Karachistan?" Huygen asked.

"Our sponsoring governments know we attacked the palace last night," Behzad replied. "Saravabad's a capital. There are embassies there. The diplomats don't know who we are or what we were doing, but you can bet they've sent word back to their governments that Nassim's palace was attacked and burned. Our people will know who did it."

"All very well, but that doesn't get us out of Karachistan.

"Right," Bolan stated. "We've got a lot of work to do."

THE EXECUTIONER SLEPT a few hours, then got ready to do a recon. You could lead a group like this straight into a guard post in the night, or you could lead them into a blind ravine and waste an hour. He'd decided during the climb the previous night that they wouldn't climb another night over land he hadn't reconnoitered.

Some of the team wanted to go with him. Especially Doug McCulloch. But the warrior said no; he was going alone.

He wore the shepherd's robe he'd worn on his recon into Saravabad, and a turban. From a little distance he might be taken for a Karachistani herdsman. Close up, no way.

The warrior left his rifle behind and carried his Beretta. As well, he clipped his knife and two grenades to the combat harness under his robe.

He began to climb. Half an hour later he faced a sheer rock face, fifty feet high. Bolan knew he couldn't get to the top without the proper equipment, so the only option was to find a way around.

It was a toss-up as to whether he went left or right. From where he stood he could see no advantage either way. He turned left.

The rock stood absolutely vertical, but at the bottom great angular rocks lay in rough heaps: what was left at the bottom of any cliff when rock broke away from the wall and fell.

Bolan imitated the walk of the scores of weary shepherds he'd seen—shuffling forward, with shoulders hunched and eyes downcast. He was uncomfortably aware that anybody on top of the rock face could see him. He stopped from time to time and stared around, wondering if an observer above would take him for a shepherd searching for a lost lamb.

The dust clouds in the alley around Saravabad indicated that mass movement was still taking place. Hoshab Nassim was moving thousands of men. Perhaps he still believed he had been attacked by thousands. Maybe he was trying to convince the foreign observers in Saravabad that he was waging war, nor just looking for a raiding party.

Bolan wondered where the man was. Had he been killed in the palace last night? Not likely, but possible. He wondered, too, about the wife of the Sudanese, the young woman now identified by Craig as an American from New Jersey. What had they done with her?

The warrior was drawn from his reverie by the sound of a "click." The sound, maybe, of a gun being cocked, of a magazine being shoved into place.

When the sound was repeated, Bolan dropped to the rocky ground, totally alert. He lay on his belly, Beretta in hand, listening, staring, trying to figure out the direction.

He heard it again, and he knew it was in front of him. Now he saw. Ahead of him someone was throwing rocks down the steep, rough mountain slope.

And then he saw why. In the shelter of a mass of rocks a little way down the slope a big black snake stood and swayed. A cobra. Somebody was trying to drive the big reptile away.

The deadly snake reared and flared. Not in the least afraid of the rocks being thrown at it—and missing by considerable distance—it defied its tormentors to come near it. Whoever those tormentors were, the cobra had their undivided attention, which made it possible for the warrior to slip a little closer and have a look.

Four members of Cobra Force had been detailed to set up an observation post. They had a pair of big binoculars and a pack radio. They had half a tent set up on poles for shade, a small machine gun stood on a bipod, set to fire down the slope—just what Bolan's group couldn't afford to confront. Just what the Executioner had probed out ahead to find.

He considered his tactical problem. The post could be taken out with one grenade. The soldiers sat together, all but casual in the shade of their half tent. One grenade in their midst would riddle them with steel pellets.

Yeah, and maybe bring a hundred of their comrades, alerted by the explosion.

They had to be taken out, but quietly. The silenced Beretta was out of the question. It would be next to impossible to down all four men without drawing return fire.

Not easy.

He worked his way uphill from them and crawled out on a ledge that overlooked the observation post. It lay beneath a steep cliff above and so guarded his back against sudden attack, and he lay and watched the soldiers throw rocks from inside the tent at the snake.

Bolan looked around at the chunks of rocks that lay all around. Some were too big to move. One was the size of a window air conditioner, and he set to work to move it near the lip of the ledge and just above the tent. Taking purchase with his boots and pushing with his shoulder, he was able to shove the rock ten feet to the edge. Next he gathered five suitcase-size rocks and lined them up behind the bigger one.

The snake down below had lost interest in the strange creatures that threw rocks at it. In all its life that venomous reptile had never seen anything it needed to be afraid of, and it wasn't afraid now. It had ceased to rear and flare and lay calmly watching the men above, its head only a little above the ground, its cold black eyes watching.

The Cobras had lost interest, too. They stopped throwing rocks. But the Executioner was still very much interested in the four Cobras.

He shoved the big rock a little to his left to line it up on the canvas that sheltered the soldiers. He checked, looking over the edge, then he sat down, put his feet against the big rock and shoved.

The rock resisted for a moment, teetered, then dropped over the edge. It had about twelve feet to fall, and it crashed down on the canvas with a blunt thud.

Bolan had stood to watch the impact. The rock had hit square in the middle of the half tent, flattening it. A man moaned. Another yelled, though feebly. A third was struggling violently to break free of the canvas.

The Executioner dropped down himself now, landing on the heels of his boots on the ground beside the shelter. Combat knife in hand, Bolan advanced. Seconds later the survivors of the "avalanche" were dead.

BOLAN CLIMBED HIGHER, putting away in his memory the turns he took, the ways he used to get around a rock face. It wouldn't be easy to find his way again with nothing but moonlight to guide him.

He began to study the mountain ridge above. Behzad had said the crest was a site for a string of Nassim's radar stations and ground-to-air missiles. Stony Man had possession of the same intel. The installations would be well guarded. He'd have to lead his group between them, staying as far away as possible.

As he climbed, he spotted the radar dish first. It was in no way camouflaged. Why should it be? Its whole function was to send out powerful beams of electromagnetic energy that identified it to anyone within a thousand miles. It stood on a steel tripod outside a concrete block control shack. The silvery antenna dish rotated, scanning the skies over Karachistan, Iran, Baluchistan, Pakistan, the Gulf of Oman.

It was one of perhaps half a dozen stations spread out over a hundred miles on the mountain ridge. More weren't needed. Missiles fired from ships in the gulf or from a neighboring country could track the signals from these radar stations and home in and destroy them in minutes. They deterred Karachistan's neighbors, but not the United States Navy.

They were there to provide the long-range radar for surface-to-air missiles. Intel was that, during the glory years of the Soviet Union, they had supplied Nassim with SA-4 Ganef missiles. Although they were now obsolete as far as the world powers were concerned, they were still formidable weapons for a country such as Karachistan. Mounted in pairs on tracked armored chassis, the Ganefs had a range of nearly fifty miles and could climb to altitudes above forty-nine thousand feet. Alerted by information from the mountaintop radar stations, their own tracking and target-acquisition radar would pick up approaching aircraft, lock on and fire. Solid-propellant boosters would launch a missile and accelerate it to a very high speed, after which the booster would drop away and the missile would fly on its own, powered by a turbo jet. The system radar would guide the missile to its target, where its explosive warhead would be detonated by a proximity fuse. Since the Ganef launchers could move at will, they were difficult to knock out.

Bolan might have liked a mission to destroy Hoshab Nassim's missile launchers—since the man was a maniacal terrorist—but that wasn't his job this time. What he had to worry about was moving his team and the liberated hostages through the line of radar stations, missile launchers and their defense detachments.

Of course, if the opportunity to knock out a Ganef launcher happened to arise...

He climbed higher and discovered that a winding road had been built along the crest of the ridge. Approaching that road, he saw that it was constantly patrolled. Military jeeps sped back and forth, as did personnel carriers and armored cars.

Crossing the road would be a challenge. Military traffic on it was so heavy that he wouldn't try it in daylight, not even alone. Terror squads, the Warden Believers and Cobra Force detachments were the essence of Nassim's regime. This mountain ridge, with its radar stations and missile launchers, was the core of his defense against the righteous wrath of his neighbors.

When Bolan looked back, he noticed that Saravabad and the valley showed less signs of moving convoys. The Karachistani forces had spent the better part of a day either trying to locate a large invasion force or trying to convince foreign observers there was such a force. Now that effort had to end.

Now they would turn to a more realistic effort: tracking down the combat team that had blasted its way into the palace compound and freed the hostages, which would make everything immensely more dangerous.

Bolan worked his way back down. With great caution he approached the observation post he'd taken out with rocks. He figured a patrol had to be coming sooner or later to find out why the post wasn't transmitting reports.

He descended via a different way, staying far away from the ledge where he had thrown the rocks. The warrior came in sight of the post, and for a couple of minutes he lay on a rock above the scene and stared down. Nothing looked different. As he crept closer, he spotted something.

Below the observation post—where flies swarmed over the bodies, buzzing in and out from under the canvas—a man lay on the ground. He had a rifle in his hands, apparently watching the approaches to the post from the valley below.

Yeah, they'd found the dead men, had known that they hadn't been killed by a rock slide and had set up pickets around the site, waiting for somebody to come back.

Well, somebody had come back. So where were the rest of them?

Bolan crawled back, into deeper cover in a cluster of rocks. For ten minutes he lay silently and waited.

But the rifleman didn't move. No man could lie on the ground for ten minutes without moving. The guy was dead.

And Bolan knew how. The guy had been the fifth man in the observation post. He'd gone down the mountainside for some reason and, coming back, he'd walked up on the cobra. The other soldiers had thrown rocks at the snake for some time. The creature was most likely agitated, and when the man stumbled on him, the cobra had struck.

The Executioner followed the path he'd remembered, alert for any reinforcements. Earlier he'd stashed away ammo, food and canteens that he'd taken from the observation post. He hurriedly gathered up the provisions from the hidden cache and went to join the others.

"WE HAVE TO THINK about something," Behzad said to Bolan as she joined him where he sat eating his rations.

"And what's that?"

"One of the hostages is a traitor. There's tension among them. They want to shoot their betrayer, but they don't know who it is."

"Craig thinks it's Barnes. Barnes thinks it's Block. What do you think?"

"It could be Barnes," she said. "Or it could be any one of the six hostages. *Any* one. Including Craig."

"Not Barnes. I've been thinking about it. It has to be someone inside the group."

She shrugged. "Could be any one of them. I wouldn't write any one of them off as innocent."

"Get all the rest you can," Bolan told the woman. "Tonight we've got to go up and over the top, which isn't going to be easy."

THEY HAD LIVED in a palace. Now they lived in what Hoshab Nassim and his Karachistani staff called a caravan, although an American would call it a house trailer or mobile home. It was drawn by a military truck, which carried the diesel-powered generator that supplied the electricity.

The trailer was air-conditioned and equipped with a bank of radio receivers and transmitters with which Nassim kept in touch with his defense force. Sauda had learned that the Karachistani army was tiny and out of favor with the dictator. They moved every few hours, mostly just along the rough road that followed the crest of the Surak Mountains, but occasionally down a few miles toward the coastal plain.

She had no idea what Nassim meant to do with her. He had imposed the chador on her, so—as he said—

his staff might not be distracted from their duties by a woman's immodesty. So she sat in the trailer, covered from head to toe in a shapeless white robe. Her ankles were still chained with the kind of leg irons she'd seen on American television when some big crook was being taken to prison. She wasn't allowed to leave the trailer. But she could look out the windows, and she spent hours staring at the sea, the blue waters of the Gulf of Oman, which she could see from the mountaintop.

She knew that the other surviving hostages had been rescued. She'd heard Nassim talking about an airborne division landing on the shores of Lake Islan. Later she heard talk of the American Rapid Deployment Force. Now it was only "the bandits," who had to be run to ground.

Hoshab Nassim stalked around his trailer, going outside only occasionally. He roared into his microphone in a language she couldn't understand. He'd put aside his white robe and wore his heavily medaled khaki uniform jacket, his jodhpurs and boots. He drank brandy and brooded.

Nassim was a megalomaniac. It was incomprehensible to him that he could make a mistake. He believed unswervingly that he was appointed by God to govern Karachistan and expand its power.

He knew, it turned out, that she was an American. He knew she was only a convert to Islam. He didn't guess, she imagined, that in her pain and hate she had changed her mind and now cared nothing for any religion; so he spoke to her of the truths of Khariji Islam, which he said he would carry to the whole Islamic world. At times he seemed to want to make a Khariji of her, maybe even to marry her. Why else would he take so much trouble to explain himself and his religion to her? But he hadn't asked her to sleep with him again, and he kept her chained. He didn't trust her.

And he damn well better not. He was the man who had murdered her husband, the man who had kept her chained and blindfolded and gagged, naked and wallowing in her own filth, for weeks. He damn well better not trust her.

She saw him strike one of his officers across the face with his riding crop and heard him order an execution. He did these things casually, as if it were his absolute right. He couldn't care less. Just as it had been his right to torture her and murder her husband. He seemed to have no idea that the officer he struck would resent it, or that she would hate him for what he had done to her. He simply had no sense of these things.

A little later he spoke to her in his halting Arabic. "The bandits are Americans, I think. They must be disappointed they did not find you. I will let them see you just before they are hanged."

12

The Executioner led the way. He had no doubts about his original team. They could make this climb, as could Barnes. Suleiman Zabara and his daughter had proved themselves capable of keeping up and carrying a fair share of the load. It was the hostages who worried Bolan.

Craig's injuries continued to hurt him. He stretched out on the ground whenever they stopped to rest, drained of color, exhausted. Even so he clung to the AK-47 assault rifle he'd taken off a dead Warden after the street fight in Saravabad. He carried it and cared for it like a soldier.

Block was a problem. He was strong and uninjured, but the steel rods shackled to his legs were increasingly painful. The shackles themselves had rubbed his flesh raw. Some of the others had worked on the locks, trying to pick them or even force them without success.

The two Russians and the Iranian and Iraqi plodded along without complaint. Although the steel bands remained around their ankles, the chain ends were tied out of their way so that the shackles didn't chafe. The men were stoic. They might, however, wind up having to carry Craig and Block on improvised litters as they had Ali.

The terrain looked different in the moonlight, but Bolan found his way, retracing his steps of the afternoon. He had long experience in matching landmarks seen in different kinds of light.

He halted the group for a rest while he went ahead and checked the observation post he'd taken out earlier. Someone had been there and removed the bodies, but hadn't established a new post. Not yet, anyway. And probably, if they had come up here in late afternoon or early evening, they hadn't taken time to investigate but had accepted what looked obvious—that the men had been crushed by a rock slide. He sent McCulloch and Huygen ahead as point men as they continued their climb.

The night was quiet. Looking back on the valley behind them, they didn't see much movement. Bolan kept watch on the mountainside above, which was where the activity had been that afternoon. The Karachistanis wouldn't defend their radar stations and missile launchers just with guard squads. No, they'd send out patrols.

By now they had to have figured that the country hadn't been invaded, that all they were looking for was a combat team and the six hostages. If Nassim had any brains at all, he'd have radically changed his strategy.

Because they had no radios and didn't dare use lights to signal, Bolan had strung out his people so that a quiet word from the front could be passed back to the others. Now a word was passed forward. It was from Sokolov, who with Bittrich was guarding the rear. "Activity behind" was what was passed on.

Bolan called his two point men to a stop and trotted back down the line. Sokolov squatted on a flat rock, looking down over the terrain they had just covered. He gave the Executioner a hand signal to keep quiet and listen.

Bolan hunkered down beside him. Yeah. The guy was right. Somebody was moving down there. You couldn't move very easily on this terrain without scraping a boot on a rock, making a sound. And this wasn't just two feet, or four. They were looking at a patrol of perhaps twenty to twenty-five men.

Bolan turned and spoke to Bittrich. "Pass the word. Everybody down and quiet."

Sokolov seized his shoulder. A bright electric light, a flashlight, shone not more than a hundred feet away.

"They're inspecting the ground," the Russian captain whispered in Bolan's ear, "tracking us. We move little rocks, expose the darker underside. They can see."

"If we have to fire on them, we're going to call down hell."

Sokolov nodded and muttered, "We might not have any choice."

Bittrich crawled back to their position. "Word passed."

The patrol picked its way forward very slowly, very cautiously. Then it stopped, lights out, and fell silent.

"It's going to hit the fan," Bolan whispered to Sokolov.

And it did. They heard a whump, which was followed by a whoosh. The patrol had a mortar.

"God!" Bittrich exclaimed.

A star shell had been fired, and it burst above the team and the hostages, flooding the rocky slope with light that seemed brighter than the brightest sunlight. And with targets in sight the Karachistani patrol opened fire.

The trained soldiers of the team—Bolan, Sokolov, McCulloch, Huygen and Bittrich—instinctively raked the downslope area with quick, short bursts of fire, enough to discourage any thought of a fast charge. Barnes had rushed forward with his Uzi, and he demonstrated his experience with the weapon by cutting down a running Karachistani with a short, accurate burst.

The star shell completely illuminated the slope, not just the part where the combat team and hostages lay, and it revealed the positions of the attack force. The Executioner pitched a grenade into the midst of the Karachistanis. Two others followed his lead, and the terrain below was alive with a deadly hail of steel pellets hurled from the grenades.

The Karachistani detachment was surprised, no doubt, at the fighting strength of the little group it had been tracking up the mountainside for the past hour. It had suffered heavy casualties, but it wasn't wiped out. The survivors returned fire, desperately fighting for their lives.

A man cried out in agony. Bolan knew that someone in his group had been hit.

The star shell burned out, and the Karachistanis used good judgment in not firing another. What they couldn't have guessed was that the SIG 550s carried by their opponents were equipped with night sights. Thinking they were safe in the dim moonlight, they had no idea that they moved about as distinct gray-green figures.

And the team began to pick them off. Four or five Karachistanis had been taken out in the opening play of the battle. About a dozen more had been killed by the grenades. Now they were being taken out one by one by mysterious deadly shooting. They began to retreat in haste.

The two men with the mortar chanced one more shot. Bolan and the others flattened themselves when they heard the round leave the tube. This was no star shell; this one was a shrapnel round. It fell short but sent a lethal wind of whining shrapnel across the front of the team's perimeter.

The Executioner spotted the mortar team through his scope and drilled one of them. The second man dropped the mortar and ran.

Firefights always seemed to last an hour and typically lasted less than a minute. This one ended, and the terrain fell silent.

Raima sobbed. Bolan supposed that meant her father had been hit, and he went to her. It wasn't her father. Suleiman knelt over someone else and prayed fervently.

The warrior knelt to see who it was. The old Muslim prayed for the soul of Robert Craig, who lay dead, shot through his chest—apparently when he rose to fire his AK-47.

"Striker!" Behzad called.

They had lost Bittrich, too. Shrapnel from the second mortar round had caught him in the throat.

"We've got to get out of here," Bolan said grimly. "They know where we are and that we can shoot back. They'll be throwing everything they've got at us."

They moved fast. There was no point in keeping quiet now. With Bolan leading, McCulloch and Huygen taking the point on the two flanks, they scrambled upward as fast as they could.

And none too fast. Struggling through narrow passes between rocks and painfully climbing steep slopes where the rocks loosened and slid down behind them, they covered fifteen hundred yards before the choppers appeared.

Ten of them. They seemed to have come from all directions. They rendezvoused, hesitating for a minute or two, as if they were planning strategy. Then they moved over the slope where the team lay and set up a close, methodical recon.

Time to hide. Every man and woman went to ground, out of sight.

Moments later the threatening helicopters swept back and forth over the slope. They used floodlights brighter than the star shell, bathing the terrain in cold white light. From time to time one of the gunners let loose a burst from a heavy-caliber weapon, firing at anything they suspected to be alive.

Bolan crouched and watched. The guns were powerful, but it was a big mountain. Probing fire or nervous fire wasn't going to hit anything. All he and his group had to do was keep their nerve and wait. The choppers, if they stayed up there long enough, would make it impossible to cross over the crest tonight, because the team wouldn't be able to move out in the open. But they wouldn't stay long. It would be a contest as to whether they would run out of gas or out of patience.

One of them came close. His floodlights—mounted on the bottom of the fuselage so their glare didn't rise and interfere with the gunners' vision—lighted the area where the team and hostages crouched. The aircraft hovered not more than a hundred feet above them, its engine roaring, its rotor beating like a great drum.

The helicopter swung around, turning its open door and machine gunner toward the clusters of rocks where the team and hostages huddled. And there it hung for a long moment, a great body swinging under its whirling rotor, the reared cobra painted on its fuselage adding to its menace.

The gunner hung forward a little over the barrels of his twin machine guns, peering down at the floodlit landscape, looking for a target. He wore a long mustache that hung down from the corners of his mouth; and, oddly for a Karachistani, no jacket or shirt. His upper body was bare and gleamed with sweat. He swung his head from side to side, staring down at the rocky mountain terrain. Then he fired, his twin machine guns drilling a steady stream of heavy rounds down among the rocks.

He hung forward and took another look—and then clutched his chest. Blood spurted between fingers, and he fell over his guns, hanging in the straps that held him in position.

Someone had broken discipline, panicked and killed the machine gunner. It had been no tough shot, but it pinpointed the team and hostages. Anyone in the helicopter knew now that a sharpshooter was directly below.

Bolan cursed.

But the chopper swung around and moved. Deafened by the clatter inside the aircraft, no one had noticed yet that the machine gunner had been shot. The chopper would cover some distance before they figured out that the man was dead.

There was time now for the team and the hostages to resume their climb. Bolan sent the order for them to press forward. "Who did it?" he asked McCulloch as the big Marine moved past him to take the point again.

"Don't know, Chief. Somebody not using their brains."

When the chopper pilot discovered his gunner was dead, he radioed the word and other helicopters converged on the area. There was no choice but to fight back. The Executioner took an Armbrust from Suleiman, who had been carrying it, and waited for a chopper to become a target.

They circled as if confused. For a few minutes Bolan thought they wouldn't come in close enough to be a big problem. Then one of them moved in, hovering almost directly above them. The gunner began to spray the ground with heavy-caliber fire, swinging the muzzles of his weapons back and forth.

Bolan raised the Armbrust and fired. The missile blasted the chopper, the explosion engulfing the aircraft in a ball of fire, then raining chunks of debris onto the mountainside.

"Now move!" Bolan yelled.

Everyone scrambled upward as the other helicopters retreated, unwilling to take the chance of being blown out of the sky. They backed away, putting a mile between themselves and the deadly soldiers on the ground.

GREATER DANGER WAITED higher on the mountain. As they climbed, Bolan and his group could hear the roar of engines above—trucks, troop carriers, armored cars. Nassim was forming a battle line along the crest of the mountain, and it would have no hundred-yard gaps.

The warrior knew he had to get his people over the crest of the mountain and well down the southern slope before daylight and, if any way possible, without the Karachistanis knowing they had crossed. Their only chance was to deceive their enemies into thinking the team was still on the northern slope, still probing for a way to get over the top.

They had just one advantage—the Karachistanis knew they had a sting. There were enough of them up above to form a line and charge down the slope, but they had too much respect for the combat team to try that. They'd wait for daylight. Then, if they thought their enemy was still on the northern slope, they'd come down with overwhelming force.

McCulloch trotted up to Bolan. "Getting awful close to it, Chief. Close enough I can hear them talking up there."

"Everybody down," Bolan said quietly, and the word was passed.

They crouched among the rocks, a hundred yards or so from the crest and the road, and it was just as McCulloch had said—they could hear voices, plus scuffling and weapons being cocked.

Bolan had just four soldiers left—himself, Sokolov, McCulloch and Huygen. Plus maybe he should count Barnes as a soldier.

Behzad was brave and strong, but she wasn't a trained soldier. Block most likely had had military training, but he was almost ineffective because of his injured legs.

Okay. He didn't have many choices. He called his team together, as well as Barnes.

"Here's what we've got to do," he said. "Make a diversion. I'm going to put some distance between me and the rest of you. Then I'll open fire and toss a grenade or two. That'll get their attention, and you'll have a good chance of crossing the road and starting down the other side. Then—"

"I think you've just offered to commit suicide," Behzad said. "Well...so. If somebody has to do it, it has to be somebody other than you, Striker. Anybody can make the noise. You must stay with us and lead. You're our most capable man. We can't escape without you."

"Look at it another way," Bolan said. "If I'm the so-called most capable man, I'm also the guy with the best chance of slipping across in the dark later. I don't plan to commit suicide. I plan to join you downhill in the morning."

"I can do it just as well as you," Sokolov told the warrior. "And she's right. We need you. I'll stay. You go."

"Look at it one more way. When you signed up for this deal, you all agreed that I give the orders, and you follow them. So I'm giving an order. You lead the group, Mikhail. I'll make the diversion. And, believe me, I'll be with you in the morning."

BOLAN HEADED EAST just below the road, doing a quick recon, judging where and how he would make his diversion.

The deal wasn't to make the diversion too far from the point where the others would cross over. He could create confusion within a radius of maybe fifty yards, a hundred at the very most. Men close to what they would think was an attack would concentrate on their own survival first, then on returning fire and turning back the assault. That would totally monopolize their attention. Men a hundred yards away wouldn't feel threatened. They'd hold their places until they got orders to move toward the attack. And they would be alert.

The Executioner's job was to put a one-minute lock on the attention of every Warden and Cobra within the radius of confusion. During that one minute, with any kind of luck at all, his people could cross the road unnoticed.

He had given them ten minutes to be in place. When hell broke loose, they were to move. Their only chance was to go within fifteen seconds of hearing his fire, run across the road and run down the south slope without looking back.

He had filled the extra magazines for his SIG 550 with the ammo he'd taken from the observation post, and clipped four grenades onto his web belt. No Armbrust. There were only two left, and the main party was more likely to need them.

The enemy was on the road above him—he could hear them talking. Occasionally he smelled the smoke from their cigarettes. He couldn't understand anything they were saying, but he could detect tension and a touch of fear in their voices.

Nine minutes. One to go.

Bolan pulled the pin on an MU 50-G hand grenade. The weapon had been designed almost as if the designer had this situation in mind. When he threw the bomb, the igniter would fire instantly—but silently and without flash or smoke, giving an observer no idea of where it had come from. When it went off, it would hurl tiny steel balls in all directions at murderous velocity, tearing into the body of anyone within fifteen or twenty feet.

When the countdown reached zero, the warrior pitched the grenade up onto the road, and in the same instant fired a burst from the SIG 550. He rolled quickly to his left and crawled a few feet, drawing his Beretta and firing the pistol in rapid succession. Then he lifted the night scope to his eye, spotted a couple of men and took them out of play with two short bursts from the SIG. He leaped to his feet and sprinted to his right, tossing another grenade on the run.

Another grenade exploded on the road. It wasn't his. And another burst of automatic fire swept across the road.

Then a man ran into the middle of the road, yelling. He proceeded to run toward the Wardens or Cobras, flailing his arms and shouting something the Executioner couldn't understand.

And then he seemed to rise into the air. A stream of slugs lifted him off his feet, then slammed him onto his face on the gravel of the road.

Wardens and Cobras scattered in gutless chaos. In the end they weren't disciplined military units, just half-disciplined gangs of terrorists and bullies. A few turned and let loose wild bursts before they dived off the far side of the road or behind a vehicle for cover. They returned no coordinated fire, organized no counterattack.

Bolan eased back down the hill. The job was done.

"Chief?" McCulloch crawled toward him.

"Corporal, your orders were to say with the main party," Bolan said curtly.

"So have me shot when we get home."

13

The Wardens and Cobras began to regroup on the road. Officers barked orders, and the troops fell in from east and west as Bolan had expected. He and McCulloch kept them off balance with an occasional burst from widely separated locations. And that was how they stumbled on Barnes, who was sitting on a low rock, laboriously stuffing 9 mm rounds into an Uzi magazine.

"You'll have to forgive me, Striker," he said without looking up. "I stumbled and didn't quite make it across the road."

No point in arguing. What was done was done, and he was there.

"Maybe you can answer me a question, then. Who ran out in the road yelling, and who took him out?"

"Kamensky," Barnes replied. "He was yelling that he was a friend of Nassim's and they shouldn't shoot him. Well, if they shouldn't, I should. And I did."

"You sure of this?" McCulloch asked, frowning.

"I understand their language, which, incidentally, you don't. It's not a good idea to be where you are and not understand a little of the lingo."

"You stayed to help us," Bolan said, a trace of doubt in his voice.

"I have another reason," Barnes replied, "and so do you."

"Let's hear it."

"Soldiering around, I've picked up a little bit of lots of languages. So I can understand a lot of what these guys say. I heard some talk from up on the road when I was on the ground, close to the pair who were talking. The dearly beloved and honored leader isn't far from here—about a mile, in a house trailer that he uses as his mobile headquarters. We got a—"

"If you're thinking about a chance to take him out, forget it," Bolan interrupted. "We didn't come to Karachistan to kill Hoshab Nassim."

"Personally I'd like to have revenge for a couple of guys," Barnes stated. "Craig, Bittrich, Sadir. Anyway, there's something else."

"I figured there would be. You have a way of having it all laid out."

"The other hostage..."

"What?"

"The Sudanese wife. Sauda Sadik, or Melanie Helms, as I'd rather think of her. She's with Nassim.

The two Cobras were making jokes about the honored great leader and his new woman.''

"Could be any woman."

"No. How many women would the honored great leader get by having their husbands shot?"

DOUG MCCULLOCH WANTED to try to rescue Melanie Helms. Gib Barnes wanted to try to kill Hoshab Nassim. Mack Bolan decided either motive was good enough to justify some risk. But for him the better motive was that an assault on the dictator's house trailer would be the ultimate diversion. Nassim would never dispatch forces into the coastal plain as long as there was a threat to his life on the crest of the Surak Mountains.

They had several hours before daylight. Bolan led the way down from the crest. He figured the Wardens and Cobras would fire some heavy-duty stuff into the area where they figured the attack had come from. And he was right.

They used their mortars to fire gas shells. Bolan guessed it was tear gas, but there was always the possibility that it was something worse. The gas was heavy and spread down the mountain slope, creeping over the ground like the artificial fog in old-time horror movies. The three men ran to keep ahead of it until soon they were as far down as the observation post Bolan had knocked out in the afternoon.

Unexpectedly the Karachistanis made a mistake. A flight of choppers flew in low over the slope, shining their lights on the rocks, and the downdraft from their rotors dissipated the gas.

McCulloch kept the helicopter crews respectful. Taking careful aim with his telescopic sight, he shot a machine gunner, then a pilot or copilot. The helicopter with the wounded pilot swung away to the west and crash-landed two hundred yards away.

"Hang in here," Bolan told his companions. "I want to check something."

He sprinted across the stony mountain slope toward the downed chopper, reaching it just as one of the machine gunners stumbled out and swung his mini-Uzi in a sweeping arc, searching for targets. Bolan took him with a quick shot from the Beretta.

The helicopter was burning, and there seemed to be no other survivors. Bolan jumped into the wreck through the wide gunner's door and looked around. The flames were hot, but it was an old Soviet chopper of the type called Horse, and Bolan had been in and out of more than his fair share over the years. He took a chance on remembering where the fire-suppression switch was.

Yeah. It was above the dead pilot's head. The Executioner pulled the switch, and the engine compartment filled with a fire-extinguishing fog.

Bolan grabbed the headphones off the corpse and pressed one to his ear. He could hear chatter. The radio was receiving. So, if it was receiving, maybe it could transmit. He picked up the microphone, keyed to transmit and began to talk.

"Zulu, Zulu, Zulu, Plan Two. Repeat, Plan Two."

He threw aside the mike and crawled out of the chopper. "Zulu" was the code name for the team, and "Plan Two" meant a pickup on the coast, not on Lake Island. Maybe nobody but Nassim's forces were listening. Chances were, though, a lot of other people were monitoring the Karachistani frequencies, especially after the attack on the palace. Even if the National Security Agency missed the transmission, the British maintained a monitoring service that covered hundreds of military, naval, police and general government frequencies. The odd "Zulu, Zulu" coming out of Karachistan might alert somebody.

Anyway, it had been worth trying.

Before leaving the chopper, which was going to burn in spite of the fire-suppressant gas he had released, Bolan took the time to detach one of the two Goryunov machine guns mounted in tandem in the side door. He looped a belt of its 7.62 mm ammunition around his neck. Slinging his SIG 550, he lugged the sixty-pound machine gun back toward his fellow soldiers.

Once back with McCulloch and Barnes he explained what he had done on the radio. "Might make the difference."

McCulloch pointed up the mountainside. "For somebody," he said. "They're getting ready to come down on us."

"We still have a big advantage," Bolan told them.

"Which is?" Barnes prompted.

"They think there's a hundred or more of us down here. What's more, with this—" he slapped the Goryunov "—we've got a way to convince them they're right."

THEY WORKED their way east. Bursts of gunfire whipped over their heads. Grenades rolled among the rocks and exploded. But everything was behind them. By moving east they'd moved beyond where the Wardens and Cobras thought they were.

The Karachistanis risked a star shell. Its cold light bore down on the terrain the three soldiers had covered a few minutes ago. They dropped to the ground among the mountain rocks and, out of sight, waited for the shell to burn itself out.

A truck stopped on the road a hundred yards or so above them. Reinforcements were silhouetted against the creamy yellow sky above the setting moon.

Bolan braced the heavy machine gun on a rock, McCulloch kneeling beside him to feed the belt, which held 250 bullets, less than half a minute's sustained firing.

But deadly firing. Bolan let loose a torrent of 7.62 mm rounds at the Wardens or Cobras who were jumping down from the truck. Slugs chopped through the swarm of men and through the canvas rear of the vehicle, drilling through many of the soldiers waiting there.

Panic. The truck sped off, leaving men lying on the road, others down and bleeding in the back.

Officers screamed orders, which galvanized the soldiers into action. They scrambled down the slope— and were caught in the fire the Cobras and Wardens hurled toward the unseen enemy below.

And that enemy had moved. It was time, Bolan judged, to climb to the road and look for Nassim's trailer.

A few moments later they reached a ditch that carried away the rainwater that fell during one of the infrequent storms that hit the area. The moon was down now, the sky an inky black.

They had sown confusion and panic, which hadn't subsided. The corpses of Wardens and Cobras littered the road. Helicopter wreckage lay on the mountainside. Bolan, McCulloch and Barnes could cross the road and go down the southern slope now. They had given Sokolov and the main party all the diversion they would need.

Now only one thing remained—to free the last hostage.

Without discussing it they moved through the ditch to the east, looking for the trailer and Hoshab Nassim.

MELANIE, AKA SAUDA, cowered on the floor of the trailer. A bullet had punched through the northern wall and out through the ceiling. God knows who had fired it.

But Nassim was furious. He threatened his subordinates with a pistol, which he pounded on the desk so hard that she was terrified it would go off. She couldn't understand what he said to the frightened officers who faced his wrath, or what he shrieked into the microphone of his radio, but he told her, in his bad Arabic, that someone had dared try to touch his exalted person and would die for it.

She didn't understand his language but had picked up a phrase, though. "Exalted person." He was an exalted person, an intimate of God, and anyone who dared touch him, or try to touch him, could only be a servant of Satan. She had decided he believed it.

The country was under attack. He was insane, beyond the slightest question, but he was in command. He sat at his radio, yelling orders into his microphone. She didn't know what he was saying, but the language had no words for some things; and she knew what he meant when he said "helicopter" or "missile."

She had wondered if he wouldn't just retreat. Now she saw he was too determined, or too insane.

She couldn't imagine what he thought. Maybe that he was invulnerable.

Whatever, the night was filled with shooting. The country had been invaded, plain enough. Watching out the window, she'd seen a helicopter burst into flame and whirl down the mountainside until it exploded on impact. Now she hugged the floor and didn't risk the windows.

Nassim stalked around, exposing himself to bullets that might fly through the thin walls of the trailer. His two personal bodyguards sat and watched him impassively, as if this kind of conduct was what was to be expected. Maybe they had seen him rant and rave too many times to be impressed anymore.

Fanatics. God save her from fanatics. Any kind.

The trailer rocked under the shock of gunfire, and Nassim shook his fist at the sky.

14

Mack Bolan crawled on eastward in the ditch by the road, followed by Barnes. McCulloch had moved several yards to the west and hurled a grenade as far as he could in that direction. The explosion created more confusion as to where the combat team was.

Vehicles sped along the narrow road in both directions, their drivers honking horns, the officers yelling, adding to the chaos.

McCulloch let loose a burst of slugs into a truck, then he scrambled back along the ditch.

After a while, the confusion began to subside. The Karachistanis began to recover their discipline and some sense or organization. They assembled in the ditch on the south side of the road and prepared to defend the road against anyone trying to cross from the north. Helicopters buzzed overhead, this time flying substantially higher. The crest of the mountain became a defensive line, and from behind the road the Cobras lobbed star shells, lighting the north side of the mountain.

A few minutes later they fired gas again. It spread out over the mountainside and crept down as before. This time the choppers stayed high and well away, learning from their past mistakes.

The gas didn't reach Bolan and his companions. The shells were detonating fifty to a hundred yards downslope, and the heavy gas didn't drift uphill.

What was more, the Karachistani defense line didn't extend far enough. It ended some fifty yards short of where the warrior and his two friends crouched in their ditch, watching. Maybe that was because three armored cars held the road just above. And maybe the armored cars were there to protect something.

Bolan crept forward, lifting his head and ducking back again, trying to get a look at what those vehicles were supposed to protect. And there it was—a long aluminum house trailer, which was attached to a military truck. In the rear of that truck, under its canvas top, an engine roared—obviously the generator. And the trailer needed a lot of electricity, from the look of the antennae on the roof.

Two more armored cars had been positioned to the east. Hoshab Nassim was well protected.

If the trio had had Armbrusts, they could have taken out the armored cars with no trouble. But that operation would have taken five Armbrusts, and they had sent the remaining two down the south slope of the mountain with the main party.

Half the belt of ammo was left for the Goryunov machine gun. A ten-second burst through that thin aluminum would take out anybody inside. But probably the female hostage was inside.

Anybody approaching the trailer would come within sight of the crews of at least two of the armored cars, the ones closest at front and rear.

Bolan settled himself in the ditch and studied the situation through the night scope of his SIG 550 assault rifle. The armored cars weren't buttoned up. It would be damn hot inside, and the crews kept the hatches open, trying to get a little air. In fact, some of the crewmen were standing outside. He could see the coiled snake emblem of Cobra Force on their sleeves.

The Executioner wondered if there was a way to draw Nassim out of that trailer. He slid back into the ditch and talked with McCulloch and Barnes. They'd make a concerted effort to generate more confusion. If it didn't work, all they could do was run. The defending forces were toughening and getting their act together. This would be the last chance to do what the three soldiers had stayed behind to do.

They lugged the Goryunov to the edge of the ditch. Barnes would man it. Bolan and McCulloch crawled away, one to the east, the other the west.

The warrior was just below the armored car nearest to the trailer, squinting through his night scope. In a moment McCulloch would be in the ditch just below the car nearest the truck. The big Marine had farther to go to get into position, so he'd fire first.

Bolan heard the rip of automatic fire and joined in. He fired and took out two crewmen who had been lounging against their armored vehicle. He leaped out of the ditch and charged across the few yards to the car, a grenade in hand. Pulling the pin, he stuffed the bomb inside the driver's hatch. A moment later the car rocked on its wheels, and two more hatches blew open from the force of the internal explosion.

Taking cover behind the car, which was beginning to burn, the warrior tossed a grenade toward the next armored vehicle. McCulloch was doing the same.

And then Barnes, on cue, opened fire with the Goryunov machine gun. The man had taken careful aim, and a torrent of 7.62 mm rounds ripped through the top of the trailer wall, then on through the roof and out into the night sky.

A fatigue-clad figure jumped from the trailer, an Uzi in hand, and began pumping slugs toward the edge of the road and the ditch. Bolan took him down with a short well-aimed burst. Another one jumped out with a grenade in hand. He, too, fell under Bolan's gunfire, and the grenade sailed over the ditch and rolled down the rocky slope before it exploded.

Barnes wasn't hit. He fired another burst through the upper wall and roof of the trailer, tearing away a large hunk of shiny aluminum. The belt ran dry.

A bearded man stepped into the doorway of the trailer and stood there, silhouetted against the bright interior lights behind him. He wore a turban and a long white robe opened in front that showed a khaki military jacket festooned with medals and ribbons. Bolan recognized him from his pictures. Hoshab Nassim just stood there, as though he defied anyone to fire a shot at him. The Executioner almost had to admire his style.

A sharp explosion detonated inside the trailer. Nassim fell forward and toppled face first into the road. A tall black woman stood behind him, a huge revolver clutched in her hand.

She couldn't walk. Her ankles were chained together by ordinary criminal leg irons, linked about twelve inches apart. She hopped down from the trailer and hobbled four or five paces onto the road before she fell.

Bolan swept her up in his arms and ran with her. When he jumped into the ditch, she fell ahead of him, scraping and bruising her arms and legs, but they made it about two seconds ahead of an angry burst of fire.

Three Wardens charged at the ditch. Barnes cut them down with a swift, efficient burst from his Uzi.

She could crawl. Bolan headed east, and she kept up with him, almost, with Barnes behind her. The chador impeded her, and she whipped it off, which left her nearly naked.

Barnes had one more grenade. He turned and pitched it back toward the trailer. The explosion and the storm of pellets cut down the first few pursuers.

The last armored car to the east began to move. It turned and started west, chopping up the ditch with machine gun fire as it came. McCulloch left the cover of a burned-out car and raced forward, jumping on the vehicle and banging on the turret hatch with the butt of his rifle. The hatch opened, and a Cobra looked out—straight into the muzzle of the Marine's Colt .45. He stared for an instant before the Colt barked and exploded his head. McCulloch armed a grenade, shoved it down the hatch and leaped. The bomb exploded, and the armored car plunged into the ditch.

In the cover of that confusion Bolan jumped up, carrying Melanie Helms over his shoulder, and sprinted across the road. In seconds he was in the ditch on the south side.

Barnes followed. McCulloch was already there.

"Now!" Bolan yelled, and while the forces above milled around and regrouped, he ran down the south slope of the mountain, hurdling rocks, stumbling, losing his balance, regaining it, carrying the woman like a wounded comrade.

Nobody fired after them. The Cobras and Wardens were still focused on the north side of the road. Looking back, the warrior could see the garish light of star shells bursting on the north side of the crest. The cannons on the armored cars fired; a dozen machine guns chattered. The Karachistanis blanketed the north slope of the mountain with everything they had.

The north slope. The wrong side of the crest. It would be some time before they realized they were firing at no one.

The soldiers and their liberated hostage had to cover as much ground as possible before the Karachistanis figured it out. Bolan slipped and fell to the ground, spilling Melanie Helms.

She rose on her knees, gasping. "Who are you?"

"Friends. We're taking you home."

She sobbed, maybe from anguish at being reminded of the death of her husband, maybe from exhaustion—likely from both.

Doug McCulloch knelt beside her. He pulled off his camouflage jacket and helped her to slip into it.

"Are you hurt?" he asked her gently.

She shook her head.

McCulloch examined her leg irons. "We can get them off when we've got some time," he said. "That *was* Nassim, wasn't it?"

She nodded. "The exalted one. Dearly beloved great leader. The man who murdered my husband."

"Okay," Bolan said, rising to his feet. "Let's keep moving."

"I'll carry her, Chief," McCulloch offered.

Bolan nodded, and the Marine picked her up like a baby in his arms.

They stumbled down the mountainside, unopposed as yet and making decent time. The helicopters arrived just before sunrise to explore the other side of the Surak Mountains.

That meant that somebody had figured it out. The enemies of Karachistan were trying to escape to the sea, to the shore of the Gulf of Oman. They must be found and destroyed.

THEY FOUND WATER. After they drank their fill and replenished their canteens, they moved on. Water attracted people. A smart searcher who knew the country would check the watering holes first.

The mountain offered a thousand deep rock crevices where a small group of people could hide. These four settled down in one of those crevices as the sun rose.

Melanie Helms—Sauda Sadik—was a beautiful young woman, Bolan decided when he had a look at her in daylight. McCulloch had decided the same, obviously. She sat on the ground, on a patch of sand the big Marine had chosen for her, with her legs stretched out before her, while he worked on her leg irons with his bayonet.

What he had in mind was to separate one of the links. To do that he put a rock between her legs, placed a link of chain on the rock and tried to force the blade into the tiny gap in the link. The link had been manufactured by bending a steel rod into the shape of a closed C. Where the two ends came around, there was a gap. McCulloch worked at trying to force the bayonet into that gap so that he could twist it and open the link.

Barnes was exhausted. He fell asleep as soon as Bolan called the halt. He'd done well for a man his age. Well for a man any age.

"I'm going to stay awake, Doug," Bolan said.

"Let me," McCulloch offered. "Till I get this damn link open, anyway. You get some sleep, Chief. I'll take first watch."

The Executioner had complete confidence in Lance Corporal Doug McCulloch. He slept easily, knowing the young man wouldn't let him down.

The sun was high when he felt the Marine nudging him and saying, "Chief, Chief, better take a look at what's going down."

Bolan was instantly alert. That was something a soldier learned: to sleep hard and fast when he could, then to be immediately awake with all senses going. He looked around and listened. And he caught what

McCulloch had meant. Choppers. There was no reason to think they'd seen anything down in this rock crevice, but they were up there, swarming.

"Sokolov and the others," McCulloch said.

Bolan nodded.

"Nothing we can do about it, I guess, but I thought you'd want to know."

Bolan was ready to ask how he'd done with the link in Melanie's chain. Then he saw that she was lying sleeping, the steel circles still locked around her ankles but the chain separated.

"Get some rest, Doug. I'll watch."

"Okay. No other activity."

The Marine sharpshooter lay down beside the sleeping young woman. She sensed his presence and moved closer to him.

Bolan climbed out of the crevice and lay on a rock to get a better look at the choppers. If they were concentrating on something, would Wardens and Cobras be far behind?

The helicopters circled, staying respectfully high. He lifted his binoculars to look at them.

Cobra choppers, with the insignia of the rearing cobra on the fuselages. Some of the machine gunners hung in harness over Goryunov machine guns. Others were behind .50-caliber guns, the weapons that could scatter a man over the landscape.

He scanned the mountainside above. Nothing. If the Cobras were coming down, they were being careful about it.

Bolan slipped back down into the crevice and sat for a while, watching the sleeping man and woman. He thought of Ali, maybe crippled for life, and he prayed to the universe that the boy was alive in the mountain village where the old doctor had promised to care for him.

And Sadir. He hadn't gotten to know Ardeshir Sadir very well, not nearly as well as you'd like to know a man who came on a mission ready to give his life for it—and did give it.

Kurt Bittrich. At one and the same time he could feel less and yet feel more about the death of Bittrich. Less because the guy had been a professional soldier and had known what might happen to him on the next mission. More because he was like Bolan, was moved by very similar incentives. Bittrich had come with his eyes open. The warrior could only be thankful the veteran soldier had died cleanly, very suddenly—one instant here, the next instant out.

Then Craig, the guy they'd come to rescue, chiefly because of what he knew. Nassim's bullyboys had tortured Craig, nearly killed him . . . and he hadn't broken.

Nassim had contempt for Americans, thought they didn't have the guts to stand up to and match the artificial courage he found in his twisted fanaticism. Craig was a guy who just worked for the government, for a modest salary, and he'd shown them the kind of courage they couldn't imagine he might have. He wasn't even a soldier. He'd fought back and died, because he was a brave man and it seemed to him like the thing to do. In Bolan's mind the world was safe as long as there were men like Robert Craig, prepared to stand and fight.

BOLAN KNELT beside Barnes and woke him.

"Gib, I want to do a little recon. Take the watch."

The older man woke more slowly than Bolan did. Even so he was soon fully alert. He stood, stretched and took a swig of water from McCulloch's canteen. He nodded, picked up his Uzi and climbed to the edge of the crevice to have a quick look around.

The Executioner climbed out and worked his way west, keeping himself down and out of sight of the choppers and anyone above.

He took stock of his ammo. He had two grenades left, about a hundred rounds for the SIG 550, twenty rounds of 9 mm. Only five shots remained in the little Walther.

Time to get careful.

If the choppers were working the mountainside to the west, they must have seen some sign of Sokolov and the others. There was no rendezvous point. Bolan had only told Sokolov that he would come down the south slope when he could. They were to look out for each other.

He worked his way carefully, slowly. The Cobras or Wardens had to be on the way. By now they had to have it figured out.

And they did.

A man who has lived his life the way the Executioner had lived his, developed finely honed instincts. More than that, he developed an ability to see and hear what other men didn't notice.

He heard the buzz of flies hovering over something that had attracted their attention. A dead sheep. Even a dead snake. What? Flies didn't gather and buzz over nothing.

He drew his Beretta and crawled toward the buzzing sound, which was joined by two or three voices, speaking in normal, casual tones.

Moments later he caught sight of a red beret, a Warden Believer, Nassim's terrorist squads. His torturers. His murderers. Bolan wondered if they knew Hoshab Nassim was dead.

He crawled toward the buzzing flies that gave him better direction than the voices. The sound, the sight of a red beret, came not from a crevice in the mountainside rocks, but from a little enclave, a deep dish among big rocks, a place hidden from the mountainside all around but not at all from choppers overhead.

One sound was a laugh.

Bolan crept out on a rock that overlooked the little bowl. And almost wished he hadn't. Not often in his experience as a soldier in the cause of justice had he been compelled to look on what he was seeing now.

Three Warden Believers squatted on the sand in the rock bowl, and in the middle, spread out naked on the sand, was the bloody corpse of Anahita Behzad.

She lay on her back, her eyes open against the sun that no longer affected them. The blood that attracted the flies came from numerous wounds that covered her body. The warrior could only guess at what she had suffered before death had claimed her.

Bolan reacted instinctively. For once, unmindful of the consequences, he pulled the pin from one of his fragmentation grenades and threw the deadly egg down among the rocks, where the three murderers sat laughing over the body of Anahita Behzad.

The explosion attracted attention. A chopper swung around and came in low to investigate the smoke and dust.

Bolan turned over on his back and raised the muzzle of the SIG 550. And he saw a missile fly up and punch into the belly of the helicopter, which erupted into a ball of flame.

15

"I don't know, Striker. I just don't know."

Mikhail Sokolov was trying to explain to Bolan how Behzad had fallen behind as they rushed down from the crest of the mountain, how he and the others had never seen her again.

"In the dark. I don't know what happened. Your diversion worked, but the Karachistanis were shooting at us just the same. A few of them. I put Colonel Ilinsky in charge of the hostages and told him to run ahead. Suleiman Zabara and Raima went with them. Jan, Anahita and I formed a rear guard to slow down pursuers. There was a lot of firing in the dark. We became separated. This morning—" He shook his head.

"They didn't just kill her," the warrior said grimly.

"Striker, I don't know if we're going to make it. Of our original eight we are only four now. We still have a long distance to go, and the enemy knows where we are."

Bolan's face was granite. "Well, we won't save ourselves by sitting here. Let's move!"

They had about another twenty miles to go until they reached the Gulf of Oman. Coming down from the Surak Mountains, they would cross farms where the Karachistanis grew wheat and some fruit and vegetables on the only really arable land in the country. It was open land, crossed by roads. The farmers and villagers would have been warned about them.

Then there was the problem of a rendezvous on the coast. They had to be spotted by some friendly unit and then picked up, either by a boat or by helicopters.

When Sokolov said he wasn't sure they could make it, he had been making a valid evaluation of the situation. Bolan wasn't so sure, either.

They reached the bottom of the mountains and the edge of the coastal plain by noon, and by then they needed rest. During the night, Block's legs had given out entirely, and this morning the men had been taking turns carrying him on a litter like they had made for Ali. Everyone was exhausted and welcomed Bolan's words that they would stop and rest. He had found a creek bed where some trees offered shade and some cover from aerial surveillance, and he sat down.

Barnes spoke now to Suleiman Zabara and Raima. They listened to him and nodded solemnly.

Barnes came and sat down beside Bolan. "I told them she's a widow now, that Hoshab Nassim is dead."

McCulloch knelt beside Melanie. He had found in someone's pack an extra pair of pants, and she had put them on. He kept trying to pick the locks on her leg irons. Although the ends of the chain hung loose from the shackles and she insisted they didn't hurt her, he kept trying.

Sokolov sat with Bolan and Barnes. "Colonel Ilinsky wants to know who Kamensky was," he said. "And why did he run yelling toward the enemy? And who shot him? And why?"

"I shot him," Barnes replied. "He was yelling at the Karachistanis that he was a friend of Nassim's so they shouldn't shoot him. He was trying to get over to the other side. Or, to put it another way, he'd been on the other side for a long time. He was our traitor."

"I don't understand," Sokolov told him.

"Let's talk with Block," Barnes suggested.

He got up and walked over to where Block lay on his litter. Bolan and Sokolov followed, and they sat down beside the Israeli intelligence agent.

"Mossad, right?" Barnes said to Block.

The man nodded weakly.

"Me, too," Barnes stated. "Not regularly. I'm not on the payroll. But I was paid by your government to try to help Sadik escape. He knew too much, and I was to kill him if I couldn't get him out. In fact, I never got a chance to do either. Nassim had him shot. I'd like to know why."

Block stared skeptically into the ruddy face of Gib Barnes. He blinked. "Nassim knew Sadik's weakness. The Warden Believers tortured her. Slowly. She didn't scream, but she wept and moaned, and Sadik could hear her. He was breaking."

"So you—" Bolan started to say.

"Not me," Block said firmly, shaking his head. "Sadik was shot by a firing squad. I can't understand why they would kill him when they had him on the point of breaking down and telling them what he knew."

"Kamensky," Bolan said.

"Incidentally," Sokolov added, "Colonel Ilinsky says Kamensky spoke Russian with a peculiar accent. He wonders if he was a Russian at all. If he was, maybe he'd been out of the country for a long time."

Barnes glanced at Melanie Helms. "Do you suppose she knows anything?"

"I'll talk to her," Bolan said.

They went over to where McCulloch was still fiddling with the young woman's leg irons and squatted beside them. "I'm sorry to have to bring this up," Bolan asked, "but do you know any more than we do about why Nassim had your husband killed?"

She nodded. "He said something about Ibrahim being of the mujahadin. He said he was lucky he was warned."

"What's the mujahadin?" McCulloch asked.

She shook her head sadly. "I don't know."

"Shiite militants," Barnes replied. "If Nassim thought Sadik was a mujahadin, he would have been afraid of him. They wanted to assassinate him and tried several times. I expect he was obsessed with them."

"So Kamensky told Nassim that Sadik was a mujahadin."

Block frowned, then nodded.

"Why?" Bolan asked.

"Maybe when Sadik talked he would have told the Wardens something Kamensky couldn't afford to have him tell," Barnes suggested.

"Like what?" Bolan asked. "What could Sadik have known?"

"Maybe that Kamensky, too, was an Israeli agent," Barnes said. "Possible, Block?"

Block shrugged. "Possible. Agents don't identify themselves to each other except when necessary. I had been told about Sadik because part of my assignment was to watch and judge him. But Kamensky..." He shrugged again.

"Chief, Trouble." McCulloch pointed at the lower slope of the mountain terrain they had just covered. At least a dozen squads of Wardens were marching down, spread out over the slope in a skirmish line.

With quick hand signals and very few words Bolan deployed his people, turning the peaceful creek bed into a defensive position. They spread out, using the ravine like a trench.

The Warden squads advanced. There was no chance they would pass by without noticing the team.

"More trouble," Huygen muttered to Bolan, nodding to the east, from which two armored cars rumbled over the fields toward the creek.

The Warden squads stopped. For a long moment they stood, uncertain, apparently, about what they should do. Then suddenly they began to break rank and retreat.

The two armored cars kept coming, moving between the creek bed and the retreating Wardens, who now broke into a run. And then the machine guns in the two armored cars opened fire and began to cut down the fleeing men.

Most of the Wardens were hit in the back as they raced away in full panic. The cars moved forward after them, guns blazing.

"My God!" Huygen muttered.

"Keep down!" Bolan yelled. "They're no friends of ours, either. They don't know we're here."

"What the hell's going on, Chief?" McCulloch asked.

"Civil war. With Nassim dead the country's falling apart."

WHICH WAS TRUE. As Bolan and the others lay in the creek bed waiting for night, they heard the sounds of battle. And when they moved out in the moonlight, they saw fires and explosions.

Two helicopters circled each other in a sort of grotesque, slow-motion dogfight until the machine gunner in one got an effective burst into the other and brought it down.

In one way it was easier to cross the last few miles to the coast. The Wardens and Cobras were focused on each other, no longer on the combat team that had come to Karachistan and assassinated Hoshab Nassim.

In another way it was more dangerous. Every armed man in Karachistan was out tonight and was shooting indiscriminately. The team came across the bodies of what had to be a farmer and his wife, probably just walking back to a village from their fields. The nearby village was burning. Why? Bolan guessed there was no reason. The country had gone crazy.

Carrying Block on his litter—for which the crippled Mossad agent kept apologizing—the group, now twelve, hurried through the night toward the coast. There were now no regular Warden stations. Nassim's terrorists squads were either fighting for their lives, were out looting or were dead.

Dead. The team and hostages came across one concrete block station, much like the one they had attacked on the mountain, that had been blasted out, apparently by cannon fire from armored cars, leaving seven Warden Believers dead in and around the ruins.

The group moved in a column. Bolan and McCulloch were out on the point; Sokolov and Huygen guarded the rear; the Iranian and Iraqi carried Block; Barnes walked to the right with his Uzi at the ready; and Colonel Ilinsky was on the left. They were a formidable little force against anything except big trouble.

But big trouble didn't come. Twice Bolan and McCulloch warned off marauders with short bursts of fire. A sustained burst of automatic fire in the night was enough to discourage small-time killers and looters. As the sun rose, they were within sight of the gulf.

In sight. And as the sun rose high, they walked down to the beach.

There was no way to signal their position. If they hid, they wouldn't be detected by friendly units at sea. If they didn't, they would be detected by unfriendly ruffians of the disorganized but still-dangerous forces of the late dictator.

The commando group walked out onto the beach on a sunlit morning, with ocean breakers rolling up the sand. They could see for miles in both directions. Fishermen worked the surf with throwing nets. The wind was fresh, smelling of saltwater.

"How'd you like to own a mile of this in a civilized country?" Barnes asked.

Bolan stood with his binoculars and scanned the horizon. In the distance he could see the shapes of great ships, indistinct in the haze over the sea. Tankers, he supposed. They had cleared the Straits of Hormuz and were on their way east.

If anybody who counted had heard the signal he'd sent from the downed helicopter, somebody had to be watching this shoreline.

His people were sitting in the sand, as though the world were a sunlit beach. But back there somewhere were thousands of men who would like nothing better than to catch up at last with the little team of soldiers that had strewn chaos over their country and caused the death of their dearly beloved leader.

Bolan stirred his people. They dug defensive and concealing positions in the sand and settled down to wait.

IN THE MIDDLE of the afternoon a gray shape loomed on the horizon, then became more distinct. A warship.

The vessel flashed a signal, finishing with the Zulu code name. Bolan grabbed for the best flashlight they had. He wasn't sure it would carry out to the ship, but he pointed it and tried. The ship stopped signaling. It had received the message.

Bolan looked through his binoculars and saw a landing craft being lowered.

"Chief..."

Bolan turned.

A strange tracked vehicle had stopped on the road just above the beach. Two jeeps pulled up near it, and men got out. They climbed onto the tracked vehicle and scanned the horizon through binoculars.

The vehicle was a Ganef missile launcher on its transporter. Although designed primarily as a surface-to-air launcher, the Ganef had been used surface-to-surface. It could damage a ship severely, just like an Exocet.

The warrior looked out to sea again. The ship had definitely launched a landing craft and was blinking its signal light again.

The Ganef crew spotted the signal, too, and the tracked vehicle turned so that its twin missiles faced out to sea. Bolan ran to Huygen, who was carrying their last Armbrust rocket. As he grabbed it and knelt to fire, the Cobras seized their weapons and opened fire on him. His soldiers returned fire instantly.

Bolan knew he had only one shot. He aimed the Armbrust at the rear quarter of the Ganef and fired. The armor-piercing missile flew hard and fast, hit the missile transporter just below the fins of the left-hand missile, penetrated the armor and exploded. Debris blown out through the top of the vehicle knocked the guidance fins off both missiles, rendering them useless. More than that, hunks of steel debris punctured the fuel tank of the left missile's ramjet engine. The fuel poured into the fire inside the transporter, and the Ganef missile exploded in a huge, smoky ball of flame.

The survivors turned tail and ran.

EPILOGUE

The Executioner leaned over for a better look at the mountain village. It was almost eternal, this kind of simple village, where for thousands of years people had led simple lives, tending their flocks and scratching a little grain out of rocky soil that begrudged their working it. Still, it had a certain beauty that made you think of uneventful lives that were hardly ever touched by political events, even the coming and going of a Hoshab Nassim.

The people had run out to stare at the big helicopter that was about to touch down. Maybe the doctor, or someone else, had told them it was coming. It was a twin-rotor transport chopper, marked with the insignia of the Red Cross and the Red Crescent.

The pilot brought it down to an easy landing on the nearest level area, some two hundred yards from the village. Bolan stood in the doorway and looked out over the approaching crowd. He spotted Ali Maquala, limping with a cane but grinning and waving. Also, right beside Ali, was the doctor who had set his ankle and arrested the gangrene that had threatened the young man's life.

The helicopter carried more than a ton of medical supplies, all the things a small hospital in a mountain village might need. It was a gift to the village from the nations that had sent the combat team to Karachistan.

Bolan held out his hand to Maquala. "I told you we'd be back."

An hour later the young Arab sat beside Bolan in the helicopter as it lifted off for a flight over the mountains and down to Kartridgabad, the former and now restored capital city of Karachistan.

Maquala had heard much on the doctor's radio, but Bolan filled him in on the mission. "We lost Ardeshir Sadir, Kurt Bittrich and Anahita Behzad. Also Bob Craig, the CIA man who was a hostage."

"But you overthrew the government!"

"Not us. It fell of its own rotten weight once Hoshab Nassim was gone."

"And the new president!"

"Yes. Suleiman Zabara, provisional president until they can hold elections."

Maquala looked back on the village, now rapidly fading in the distance. "I will come back here. I . . . I wish to marry."

"You didn't waste any time."

The young man frowned. "I am especially sorry to learn of the death of Anahita."

Bolan nodded. "She was brave."

Maquala was silent for a moment. "Who shot Nassim?"

"One of the hostages, the wife of the Sudanese. She's an American."

"Ahh..."

When the big chopper landed at Kartridgabad, some of the team and the hostages were waiting on the helicopter pad. Mikhail Sokolov had already flown to Moscow, but Jan Huygen stood on the tarmac, grinning, as did Gib Barnes. Nathan Block stood on crutches.

Bolan looked around for Doug McCulloch, then he spotted him trotting across the grass toward the pad. Melanie Helms was with him. They held hands.

Bolan wasn't good with goodbyes. He shook hands all around before he boarded the Navy helicopter that would fly him out to a carrier, from where he would be flown by jet to Washington. Hal Brognola had another mission lined up for him.

That was how it always was. The battle might be won, but not the war. With a final word of thanks and a curt nod the Executioner turned and was gone.

DON PENDLETON's

MACK BOLAN®

More of the best in paramilitary adventure!

FIREPOWER $4.99   ☐
The American defense industry has been dealt a deadly
blow. Dirty men with dirty money are out for the kind of
control that breaches national security. Bolan finds
himself in the middle of a war with no clear line of fire.

STORM BURST $4.99   ☐
In the final installment of the Storm Trilogy, Mack Bolan
faces an Arab-Soviet conspiracy terrorizing the free
world. The Executioner races to prevent a nuclear
showdown that threatens to explode—literally—across
the globe.

INTERCEPT $4.99   ☐
What civilization has feared the most since Hitler is
about to happen: deadly technology reaching the
hands of a madman. All he needs to complete his
doomsday weapon is a missing scrambler component.
The only thing standing in his way is The Executioner.

Total Amount	$ _____
Plus 75¢ Postage ($1.00 in Canada)	_____
Canadian residents add applicable federal and provincial taxes	
Payment Enclosed	$ _____

If you missed any of these titles, please send a check or money order, payable to Gold
Eagle Books, to:

In the U.S.

Gold Eagle Books
3010 Walden Avenue
P.O. Box 1325
Buffalo, NY 14269-1325

In Canada

Gold Eagle Books
P.O. Box 609
Fort Erie, Ontario
L2A 5X3

Please Print

Name:_____

Address:_____

City:_____

State/Prov:_____

Zip/Postal Code:_____

SBBL

Dan Samson finds himself a deciding factor in the Civil War in the third thrilling episode of the action miniseries...

TIMERAIDER

John Barnes

Dan Samson, a hero for all time, is thrown into the past to fight on the battlefields of history.

In Book 3: UNION FIRES, the scene has switched to the Civil War, and Vietnam veteran Dan Samson works to free a leading member of the biggest resistance group in the South.

Available in December at your favorite retail outlet.

To order Book 1: WARTIDE, Book 2: BATTLECRY or Book 3: UNION FIRES, please send your name, address, zip or postal code, along with a check or money order (please do not send cash) for $3.50 for each book ordered, plus 75¢ postage and handling ($1.00 in Canada), payable to Gold Eagle Books to:

In the U.S.

Gold Eagle Books
3010 Walden Avenue
P.O. Box 1325
Buffalo, NY 14269-1325

In Canada

Gold Eagle Books
P.O. Box 609
Fort Erie, Ontario
L2A 5X3

GOLD
EAGLE ®

Please specify book title(s) with your order.
Canadian residents add applicable federal and provincial taxes.

TR3

In the 21st century, a new breed of cop brings home the law in the latest installment of the future law-enforcement miniseries...

CADE

MIKE LINAKER

In the 21st-century nightmare, marshals like Thomas Jefferson Cade carry a badge, a gun and a burning sense of justice.

In Book 3: FIRESTREAK, Cade and his cyborg partner, Janek, follow the bloody trail of a renegade drug dealer to the electronic wonderland of Los Angeles and enter the killzone... guns loaded, targets in sight.

Available in January at your favorite retail outlet.

To order Book 1: DARKSIDERS, Book 2: HARDCASE or Book 3: FIRESTREAK, please send your name, address, zip or postal code, along with a check or money order (please do not send cash) for $3.50 for each book ordered, plus 75¢ postage and handling ($1.00 in Canada), payable to Gold Eagle Books to:

In the U.S.

Gold Eagle Books
3010 Walden Avenue
P.O. Box 1325
Buffalo, NY 14269-1325

In Canada

Gold Eagle Books
P.O. Box 609
Fort Erie, Ontario
L2A 5X3

Please specify book title(s) with your order.
Canadian residents add applicable federal and provincial taxes.

GOLD
EAGLE ®

CADE3

Raw determination
in a dark new age.

JAMES AXLER

DEATH LANDS®

Fury's Pilgrims

A bad jump from a near-space Gateway leaves Ryan Cawdor and his band
of warrior survivalists in the devastated heart of the American Midwest.
In a small community that was once the sprawling metropolis of Chi-
cago, Krysty is taken captive by a tribe of nocturnal female mutants. Ryan
fears for her life, especially since she is a woman.

In the Deathlands, life is a contest where the only victor is death.

Available in January at your favorite retail outlet, or order your copy now by sending your
name, address, zip or postal code along with a check or money order (please do not send
cash) for $4.99 for each book ordered, plus 75¢ postage and handling ($1.00 in Canada),
payable to Gold Eagle Books, to:

In the U.S.

Gold Eagle Books
3010 Walden Avenue
P.O. Box 1325
Buffalo, NY 14269-1325

In Canada

Gold Eagle Books
P.O. Box 609
Fort Erie, Ontario
L2A 5X3

GOLD
EAGLE ®

Please specify book title with order.
Canadian residents add applicable federal and provincial taxes.

DL-17

Gold Eagle brings another fast-paced miniseries to the action adventure front!

by PATRICK F. ROGERS

Omega Force: the last—and deadliest—option

With capabilities unmatched by any other paramilitary organization in the world, Omega Force is a special ready-reaction anti-terrorist strike force composed of the best commandos and equipment the military has to offer.

In Book 1: **WAR MACHINE**, two dozen SCUDs have been smuggled into Libya by a secret Iraqi extremist group whose plan is to exact ruthless retribution in the Middle East. The President has no choice but to call in Omega Force—a swift and lethal way to avert World War III.

WAR MACHINE, Book 1 of this three-volume miniseries, hits the retail stands in February, or order your copy now by sending your name, address, zip or postal code, along with a check or money order (please do not send cash) for $3.50, plus 75¢ postage and handling ($1.00 in Canada), payable to Gold Eagle Books, to:

In the U.S.	In Canada
Gold Eagle Books	Gold Eagle Books
3010 Walden Avenue	P.O. Box 609
P.O. Box 1325	Fort Erie, Ontario
Buffalo, NY 14269-1325	L2A 5X3

Please specify book title with your order.
Canadian residents add applicable federal and provincial taxes.

GOLD EAGLE®

OM1